D1343546

Please return/renew this item by the last date shown

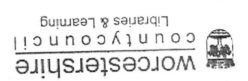

worcestershire
countycouncil
Libraries & Learning

ALSO BY PHILIP ROTH

ZUCKERMAN BOOKS

The Ghost Writer
Zuckerman Unbound
The Anatomy Lesson
The Prague Orgy
The Counterlife
American Pastoral
I Married a Communist
The Human Stain
Exit Ghost

ROTH BOOKS

The Facts • Deception
Patrimony • Operation Shylock
The Plot Against America

KEPESH BOOKS

The Breast
The Professor of Desire
The Dying Animal

MISCELLANY

Reading Myself and Others
Shop Talk

OTHER BOOKS

Goodbye, Columbus • Letting Go
When She Was Good • Portnoy's Complaint • Our Gang
The Great American Novel • My Life as a Man
Sabbath's Theater • Everyman • Indignation

PHILIP ROTH

The Humbling

VINTAGE BOOKS

London

Published by Vintage 2010

2 4 6 8 10 9 7 5 3 1

Copyright © Philip Roth 2009

Philip Roth has asserted his right under the Copyright, Designs and
Patents Act 1988 to be identified as the author of this work

This book is sold subject to the condition that it shall not,
by way of trade or otherwise, be lent, resold, hired out,
or otherwise circulated without the publisher's prior
consent in any form of binding or cover other than that
in which it is published and without a similar condition,
including this condition, being imposed on the
subsequent purchaser

First published in Great Britain in 2009 by Jonathan Cape

Vintage
Random House, 20 Vauxhall Bridge Road,
London SW1V 2SA

www.randomhouse.co.uk

Addresses for companies within The Random House Group Limited
can be found at: www.randomhouse.co.uk/offices.htm

The Random House Group Limited Reg. No. 954009

A CIP catalogue record for this book
is available from the British Library

ISBN 9780099535652

The Random House Group Limited supports The Forest
Stewardship Council (FSC), the leading international forest
certification organisation. All our titles that are printed on
Greenpeace approved FSC certified paper carry the FSC logo.
Our paper procurement policy can be found at:
www.rbooks.co.uk/environment

Mixed Sources
Product group from well-managed
forests and other controlled sources
www.fsc.org Cert no. TT-COC-2139
© 1996 Forest Stewardship Council

Printed and bound in Great Britain by
CPI Bookmarque, Croydon, CR0 4TD

For J. T.

The Humbling

1

Into Thin Air

He'd lost his magic. The impulse was spent.
He'd never failed in the theater, everything he had
done had been strong and successful, and then the
terrible thing happened: he couldn't act. Going onstage became agony. Instead of the certainty that
he was going to be wonderful, he knew he was going to fail. It happened three times in a row, and by
the last time nobody was interested, nobody came.
He couldn't get over to the audience. His talent was
dead.

Of course, if you've had it, you always have
something unlike anyone else's. I'll always be unlike
anyone else, Axler told himself, because I am who
I am. I carry that with me—that people will always
remember. But the aura he'd had, all his manner-
isms and eccentricities and personal peculiarities,

what had worked for Falstaff and Peer Gynt and Vanya—what had gained Simon Axler his reputation as the last of the best of the classical American stage actors—none of it worked for any role now. All that had worked to make him himself now worked to make him look like a lunatic. He was conscious of every moment he was on the stage in the worst possible way. In the past when he was acting he wasn't thinking about anything. What he did well he did out of instinct. Now he was thinking about everything, and everything spontaneous and vital was killed—he tried to control it with thinking and instead he destroyed it. All right, Axler told himself, he had hit a bad period. Though he was already in his sixties, maybe it would pass while he was still recognizably himself. He wouldn't be the first experienced actor to go through it. A lot of people did. I've done this before, he thought, so I'll find some way. I don't know how I'm going to get it this time, but I'll find it—this will pass.

It didn't pass. He couldn't act. The ways he could once rivet attention on the stage! And now he dreaded every performance, and dreaded it all day long. He spent the entire day thinking thoughts he'd never thought before a performance in his life:

I won't make it, I won't be able to do it, I'm playing the wrong roles, I'm overreaching, I'm faking, I have no idea even of how to do the first line. And meanwhile he tried to occupy the hours doing a hundred seemingly necessary things to prepare: I have to look at this speech again, I have to rest, I have to exercise, I have to look at that speech again, and by the time he got to the theater he was exhausted. And dreading going out there. He would hear the cue coming closer and closer and know that he couldn't do it. He waited for the freedom to begin and the moment to become real, he waited to forget who he was and to become the person doing it, but instead he was standing there, completely empty, doing the kind of acting you do when you don't know what you are doing. He could not give and he could not withhold; he had no fluidity and he had no reserve. Acting became a night-after-night exercise in trying to get away with something.

It had started with people speaking to him. He couldn't have been more than three or four when he was already mesmerized by speaking and being spoken to. He had felt he was in a play from the outset. He could use intensity of listening, concentration, as lesser actors used fireworks. He had that power offstage, too, particularly, when younger, with women who did not realize that they had a story until he revealed to them that they had a story, a voice, and a style belonging to no other. They became actresses with Axler, they became the heroines of their own lives. Few stage actors could speak and be spoken to the way he could, yet he could do neither anymore. The sound that used to go into his ear felt as though it were going out, and every word he uttered seemed acted instead of spoken. The initial source in his acting was in what he heard, his response to what he heard was at the core of it, and if he couldn't listen, couldn't hear, he had nothing to go on.

He was asked to play Prospero and Macbeth at the Kennedy Center—it was hard to think of a more ambitious double bill—and he failed appallingly in both, but especially as Macbeth. He couldn't do low-intensity Shakespeare and he couldn't do high-intensity Shakespeare—and he'd been doing Shakespeare all his life. His Macbeth was ludicrous and everyone who saw it said as much, and so did many who hadn't seen it. "No, they don't even have to have been there," he said, "to insult you." A lot of actors would have turned to drink to help themselves out; an old joke had it that there was an actor who would always drink before he went onstage, and when he was warned "You mustn't drink," he replied, "What, and go out there alone?" But Axler didn't drink, and so he collapsed instead. His breakdown was colossal.

The worst of it was that he saw through his breakdown the same way he could see through his acting. The suffering was excruciating and yet he doubted that it was genuine, which made it even worse. He did not know how he was going to get from one minute to the next, his mind felt as though it were melting, he was terrified to be alone, he could not sleep more than two or three hours a night, he scarcely ate, he thought every day of killing himself with the gun in the attic—a Remington 870 pump-action shotgun that he kept in the isolated farmhouse for self-defense—and still the whole thing seemed to be an act, a bad act. When you're playing the role of somebody coming apart, it has organization and order; when you're observing yourself coming apart, playing the role of your own demise, that's something else, something awash with terror and fear.

He could not convince himself he was mad any

more than he'd been able to convince himself or anyone else he was Prospero or Macbeth. He was an artificial madman too. The only role available to him was the role of someone playing a role. A sane man playing an insane man. A stable man playing a broken man. A self-controlled man playing a man out of control. A man of solid achievement, of theatrical renown—a large, burly actor standing six feet four inches tall, with a big bald head and the strong, hairy body of a brawler, with a face that could convey so much, a decisive jaw and stern dark eyes and a sizable mouth he could twist every which way, and a low commanding voice emanating from deep down that always had a little growl in it, a man conscientiously on the grand scale who looked as if he could stand up to anything and easily fulfill all of a man's roles, the embodiment of invulnerable resistance who looked to have absorbed into his being the egoism of a dependable giant—playing an insignificant mite. He screamed aloud when he awakened in the night and found himself still locked inside the role of the man deprived of himself, his talent, and his place in the world, a loathsome man who was nothing more than the inventory of his defects. In the mornings he hid in bed for hours, but instead of hiding from the role he was merely playing the role. And when finally he got up, all he could think about was suicide, and not its simulation either. A man who wanted to live playing a man who wanted to die.

Meanwhile, Prospero's most famous words wouldn't let him be, perhaps because he'd so recently mangled them. They repeated themselves so regularly in his head that they soon became a hubbub of sounds tortuously empty of meaning and pointing at no reality yet carrying the force of a spell full of personal significance. "Our revels now are ended. These our actors, / As I foretold you, were all spirits and / Are melted into air, into thin air." He could do nothing to blot out "thin air," the two syllables that were chaotically repeated while he lay powerless in his bed in the morning and that had the aura of an obscure indictment even as they came to make less and less sense. His whole intricate personality was entirely at the mercy of "thin air."

VICTORIA, Axler's wife, could no longer care for him and by now needed tending herself. She would cry whenever she saw him at the kitchen table, his head in his hands, unable to eat the meal she had prepared. "Try something," she begged, but he ate nothing, said nothing, and soon Victoria began to panic. She had never seen him give way like this before, not even eight years earlier when his elderly parents had died in an automobile crash with his father at the wheel. He wept then and he went on. He always went on. He took the losses hard but the performance never faltered. And when Victoria was in turmoil, it was he who kept her tough and got her through. There was always a drug drama with her errant son. There was the permanent hardship of aging and the end of her career. So much disappointment, but he was there and so she could bear it. If only he were here now that the man on whom she had depended was gone!

In the 1950s, Victoria Powers had been Balanchine's youngest favorite. Then she hurt her knee, had an operation, danced again, hurt it again, had another operation, and by the time she was rehabilitated the second time round, someone else was Balanchine's youngest favorite. She never recovered her place. There was a marriage, the son, a divorce, a second marriage, a second divorce, and then she met and fell in love with Simon Axler, who, when he'd first come from college two decades earlier to make a career on the New York stage, used to go to the City Center to see her dance, not because he loved ballet but because of his youthful susceptibility to the capacity she had to stir him to lust through the pathway of the tenderest emotions: she remained in his memory for years afterward as the very incarnation of erotic pathos. When they met as forty-year-olds in the late seventies, it was a long time since anyone had asked her to perform, though pluckily she went off every day to her workout at a local dance studio. She had done all she could to keep herself fit and looking youthful, but by then her pathos exceeded any ability she'd ever had to master it artistically.

After the Kennedy Center debacle and his unexpected collapse, Victoria fell apart and fled to California to be close to her son.

ALL AT ONCE Axler was alone in the house in the country and terrified of killing himself. Now there was nothing stopping him. Now he could go ahead and do what he'd found himself unable to do while she was still there: walk up the stairs to the attic, load the gun, put the barrel in his mouth, and reach down with his long arms to pull the trigger. The gun as the sequel to the wife. But once she'd left, he didn't make it through the first hour alone—didn't even go up the first flight of stairs toward the attic —before he had phoned his doctor and asked him to arrange for his admission to a psychiatric hospital that very day. Within only minutes the doctor had found him a place at Hammerton, a small hospital with a good reputation a few hours to the north.

He was there for twenty-six days. Once interviewed, unpacked, relieved of his "sharps" by a nurse, and his valuables taken to the business office for safekeeping, once alone and in the room assigned him, he sat down on the bed and remembered role after role that he had played with absolute assurance since he'd become a professional in his early twenties—what had destroyed his confidence now? What was he doing in this hospital room? A self-travesty had come into being who did not exist before, a self-travesty grounded in nothing, and he was that self-travesty, and how had it happened? Was it purely the passage of time bringing on decay and collapse? Was it a manifestation of aging? His appearance was still impressive. His

aims as an actor had not changed nor had his pain-
staking manner of preparation for a role. There was
no one more thorough and studious and serious, no
one who took better care of his talent or who better
accommodated himself to the changing conditions
of a career in the theater over so many decades. To
cease so precipitously being the actor he was—it
was inexplicable, as though he'd been disarmed of
the weight and substance of his professional existence one night while he slept. The ability to speak
and be spoken to on a stage—that's what it came
down to, and that's what was gone.

The psychiatrist he saw, Dr. Farr, questioned
whether what had befallen him could truly be cause-
less, and in their twice-weekly sessions asked him to
examine the circumstances of his life preceding the
sudden onset of what the doctor described as "a
universal nightmare." By this he meant that the actor's misfortune in the theater—going out on the
stage and finding himself unable to perform, the
shock of that loss—was the content of troubling
dreams any number of people had about themselves, people who, unlike Simon Axler, were not
professional actors. Going out on the stage and being unable to perform was among the stock set of

dreams that most every patient reported at one
time or another. That and walking naked down a
busy city street or being unprepared for a crucial
exam or falling off a cliff or finding on the highway
that your brakes don't work. Dr. Farr asked Axler to
talk about his marriage, about his parents' death,
about his relations with his drug-addicted stepson,
his boyhood, his adolescence, his beginnings as an
actor, an older sister who had died of lupus when he
was twenty. The doctor wanted to hear in particu-
lar detail about the weeks and months leading up to
his appearance at the Kennedy Center and to know
if he remembered anything out of the ordinary,
large or small, occurring during that period. Axler
worked hard to be truthful and thereby to reveal
the origins of his condition—and with that to recover his powers—but as far as he could tell, no
cause for the "universal nightmare" presented itself
in anything he said sitting across from the sympa-
thetic and attentive psychiatrist. And that made it
all the more a nightmare. Yet he talked to the doctor anyway, each time he showed up. Why not? At
a certain stage of misery, you'll try anything to explain what's going on with you, even if you know it

doesn't explain a thing and it's one failed explanation after another.

Some twenty days into his stay at the hospital a night came when, instead of waking at two or three and lying sleepless in the midst of his terror till dawn, he slept right through until eight in the morning, so late by hospital standards that a nurse had to come to his room to awaken him so that he could join the other patients for 7:45 breakfast in the dining hall and then begin the day, which included group therapy, art therapy, a consultation with Dr. Farr, and a session with the physical therapist, who was doing her best to treat his perennial spinal pain. Every waking hour was filled with activities and appointments to prevent the patients from retiring to their rooms to lie depressed and miserable on their beds or to sit around with one another, as a number of them did in the evenings anyway, discussing the ways they had tried to kill themselves.

Several times he sat in the corner of the rec room with the small gang of suicidal patients and listened to them recalling the ardor with which they had planned to die and bemoaning how they had failed.

Each of them remained immersed in the magnitude of his or her suicide attempt and the ignominy of having survived it. That people could really do it, that they could control their own death, was a source of fascination to them all—it was their natural subject, like boys talking about sports. Several described feeling something akin to the rush that a psychopath must get when he kills someone else sweeping over them when they attempted to kill themselves. A young woman said, "You seem to yourself and to everyone around you paralyzed and wholly ineffectual and yet you can decide to commit the most difficult act there is. It's exhilarating. It's invigorating. It's euphoric." "Yes," said someone else, "there's a grim euphoria to it. Your life is falling apart, it has no center, and suicide is the one thing you can control." One elderly man, a retired schoolteacher who had tried to hang himself in his garage, gave them a lecture on the ways "outsiders" think about suicide. "The one thing that everyone wants to do with suicide is explain it. Explain it and judge it. It's so appalling for the people that are left behind that there has to be a way of thinking about it. Some people think of it as an act of cowardice. Some people think of it as criminal, as a crime

against the survivors. Another school of thought
finds it heroic and an act of courage. Then there
are the purists. The question for them is: was it jus-
tified, was there sufficient cause? The more clinical
point of view, which is neither punitive nor idealiz-
ing, is the psychologist's, which attempts to de-
scribe the state of mind of the suicide, what state of
mind he was in when he did it." He went tediously
on in this vein more or less every night, as though
he were not an anguished patient like the rest of
them but a guest lecturer who'd been brought in
to elucidate the subject that obsessed them night
and day. One evening Axler spoke up—to perform,
he realized, before his largest audience since he'd
given up acting. "Suicide is the role you write for
yourself," he told them. "You inhabit it and you en-
act it. All carefully staged—where they will find you
and how they will find you." Then he added, "But
one performance only."

In their conversation, everything private was revealed easily and shamelessly; suicide seemed like
a very huge aim and living a hateful condition.
Among the patients he met, there were some who
knew him right off because of his handful of movies,
but they were too immersed in their own struggles

to take much more notice of him than they did of anyone other than themselves. And the staff was too busy to be distracted for long by his theatrical renown. He was all but unrecognizable in the hospital, not only to others but to himself.

From the moment that he had rediscovered the miracle of a night's sleep and had to be awakened for breakfast by the nurse, he began to feel the dread subside. They had given him one medication for depression that didn't agree with him, then a second, and finally a third that caused no intolerable side effects, but whether it did him any good, he could not tell. He could not believe that his improvement had anything to do with pills or with psychiatric consultations or group therapy or art therapy, all of which felt like empty exercises. What continued to frighten him, as the day of his discharge approached, was that nothing that was happening to him seemed to have to do with anything else. As he'd told Dr. Farr—and further convinced himself by having tried to the best of his ability to search for a cause during their sessions—he had lost his magic as an actor for no good reason and it was just as arbitrarily that the desire to end his life began to ebb, at least for the time being. "*Nothing* has a good reason for happening," he said to the doctor later that day. "You lose, you gain—it's all caprice. The omnipotence of caprice. The likelihood of reversal. Yes, the unpredictable reversal and its power."

Near the end of his stay he made a friend, and each night they had dinner together she repeated her story to him. He had met her first in art therapy, and after that they would sit across from each other at a table for two in the dining hall, chatting like a couple on a date, or—given the thirty-year age difference—like a father and daughter, albeit about her suicide attempt. The day they met—a couple of days after her arrival—there had been only the two of them in the art room along with the therapist, who, as though they were kindergarteners, had handed each sheets of white paper and a box of crayons to play with and told them to draw whatever they wanted. All that was missing from the room, he thought, were the little tables and chairs. To satisfy the therapist, they worked in silence for fifteen minutes and then, again for the sake of the therapist, listened attentively to the response each offered to the other's drawing. She had drawn a house and a garden, and he a picture of himself drawing a picture, "a picture," he told the therapist when she asked him what he'd done, "of a man who has broken down and who commits himself to a psychiatric hospital and goes to art therapy and is asked there by the therapist to draw a picture." "And suppose you were to give your picture a title, Simon. What would it be?" "That's easy. 'What the Hell Am I Doing Here?'"

The five other patients scheduled to be at art therapy either were back on their beds, unable to do anything except lie there and weep, or, as though an emergency had befallen them, had rushed off without an appointment to their doctors' offices and were sitting in the waiting room preparing to lament over the wife, the husband, the child, the boss, the mother, the father, the boyfriend, the girl-friend—whomever it was they never wanted to see again, or whom they would be willing to see again so long as the doctor was present and there was no shouting or violence or threats of violence, or whom they missed horribly and couldn't live without and whom they would do anything to get back. Each of them sat waiting a turn to denounce a parent, to vilify a sibling, to belittle a mate, to vindicate or excoriate or pity themselves. One or two of them who could still concentrate—or pretend to concentrate, or strain to concentrate—on something other than the misery of their grievance would, while waiting for the doctor, leaf through a copy of *Time* or *Sports Illustrated* or pick up the local paper and try to do the crossword puzzle. Everybody else would be sitting there gloomily silent, inwardly intense and rehearsing to themselves—in the lexicon of pop psychology or gutter obscenity or Christian suffering or paranoid pathology—the ancient themes of dramatic literature: incest, betrayal, injustice, cruelty, vengeance, jealousy, rivalry, desire, loss, dishonor, and grief.

She was an elfin, pale-skinned brunette with the bony frailty of a sickly girl of about a quarter her age. Her name was Sybil Van Buren. In the eyes of the actor hers was a thirty-five-year-old body that not only refused to be strong but dreaded even the appearance of strength. And yet, for all her delicacy, she'd said to him, on the way up the path to the main residence hall from art therapy, "Will you eat dinner with me, Simon?" Amazing. Still some kind of wish in her not to be swallowed up. Or maybe she'd asked to stay on at his side in the hope that with a little luck something would ignite between them that would complete the doing in of her. He was big enough for the job, more than whale enough for a tiny bundle of flotsam like her. Even here—where, without assistance from the pharmacopoeia, any show of stability, let alone bravado, was unlikely to quell for long the maelstrom of terror swirling back of the gullet—he had not lost the loose, swaggering gait of the ominous man that had once gone toward making him such an original Othello. And so, yes, if there was still any hope for her of going completely under, perhaps it lay in cozying up to him. That's what he thought at the outset anyway.

"I had lived for so long in the constraints of caution," Sybil told him at dinner that first night. "The efficient housewife who gardens and sews and can repair everything and throws glorious dinner parties as well. The quiet, steady, loyal sidekick of the rich and powerful man, with her unambiguous, wholehearted, old-fashioned devotion to the rearing of children. The ordinary existence of an insignificant mortal. Well, I went off to go shopping for groceries—what could be more mundane than that? Why would anyone in the world have to worry about that? I'd left my daughter playing out back in the yard and our little boy upstairs sleeping in his crib and my rich and powerful second husband watching a golf tournament on TV. I turned around and came home because when I got to the supermarket I realized I'd forgotten my wallet. The little one was still sleeping. And in the living room the golf game was still going, but my eight-year-old daughter, my little Alison, was sitting up on the sofa without her underpants and my rich and powerful second husband was kneeling on the floor, his head between her plump little legs."

"What was he doing there?"

"What men do there."

Axler watched her cry and said nothing.

"You've seen my artwork," she finally told him. "The sun shining down on a pretty house and the garden all in bloom. You know me. *Everybody* knows me. I think the best of everything. I prefer it that way and so does everyone around me. He got up off his knees, completely unruffled, and told me that she had been complaining about an itch and she wouldn't stop scratching herself, and so, before she did herself any harm, he had taken a look to be sure she was all right. And she was, he assured me. He could see nothing, not a blemish, not a sore, not a rash . . . She was fine. 'Good,' I said. 'I came back for my wallet.' And instead of getting his hunting rifle from the basement and pumping him full of bullets, I found my wallet in the kitchen, said 'Bye again, everyone,' and went off to the store as if what I had witnessed was a commonplace occurrence. In a daze, dumbfounded, I filled two shopping carts. I would have filled two more, four more, six more if the store manager hadn't seen me blubbering away and come over to ask if I was all right. He drove me home in his car. I left our car in the lot there and was driven home. I couldn't negotiate the stairs. I had to be carried up to bed. There I lay for four days, unable to speak or eat, barely able to drag myself to the bathroom. The story was that I'd come down with a fever and been ordered to bed. My rich and powerful second husband could not have been more solicitous. My little darling Alison sweetly brought me a vase of cut flowers from my garden. I could not ask her, I could not bring myself to say, 'Who removed your underpants? What do you want to tell me? If you really had some kind of itch, you would have waited, wouldn't you, until I came home from shopping to show me? But, dear, if you didn't have an itch . . . dear, if there's something you're not telling me because you're afraid to . . . ?' But I was the one who was afraid. I could not do it. By the fourth day I had convinced myself that I had imagined everything, and two weeks later, when Alison was at school and he was at work and the little one was taking his nap, I got out the wine and the Valium and the plastic garbage bag. But I couldn't stand suffocating. I panicked. I took the pills and the wine but then I remember not getting any air and hurrying to rip the bag off. And I don't know what I regret more horribly—having tried to do it or having failed to do it. All I want to do is shoot him. Only now he's alone with them and I'm here. He's all alone with my sweet little girl! It can't be! I called my sister and asked her to stay at the house with them, but he wouldn't let her sleep there. He said there was no need. And so she left. And what can I do? I'm here and Alison's there! I was paralyzed! I did nothing that I should have done! Nothing that anyone would have done! I should have rushed the child to the doctor! I should have called the police! It was a criminal act! There are laws against such things! Instead I did nothing! But he said nothing had happened, you see. He says that I'm hysterical, that I'm deluded, that I'm mad

—but I'm not. I swear to you, Simon, I'm not mad. *I saw him doing it.*"

"That's horrible. A horrible transgression," Axler said. "I see why it's done what it did to you."

"It's *evil*. I need someone," she confided in a murmur, "to kill this evil man."

"I'm sure you could find a willing party."

"You?" asked Sybil in a tiny voice. "I'd pay."

"If I was a killer I would do it pro bono," he said, taking the hand she extended to him. "People become infected with the rage when an innocent child is violated. But I'm an out-of-work actor. I'd botch the job and we'd both go to jail."

"Oh, what should I do?" she asked him. "What would you do?"

"Get strong. Cooperate with the doctor and try to get strong as fast as you can so you can go home to your children."

"You believe me, don't you?"

"I'm sure you saw what you saw."

"Can we have dinner together?"

"For as long as I'm here," he said.

"I knew in art therapy that you'd understand. There's so much suffering in your eyes."

Within months of his leaving the hospital, his

wife's son died of an overdose and the marriage of the occupationless dancer to the occupationless actor ended in divorce, completing yet one more of the many millions of stories of unhappily entwined men and women.

ONE DAY AROUND NOON a black town car pulled into the driveway and parked beside the barn. It was a chauffeur-driven Mercedes and the small white-haired man who stepped out of the back seat was Jerry Oppenheim, his agent. After the hospital internment, Jerry had phoned him every week from New York to see how he was doing, but many months had gone by without their speaking—the actor having chosen at one point to stop taking the agent's calls along with most everyone else's—and the visit was unexpected. He watched Jerry, who was over eighty and walked cautiously, negotiate the stone path to the front door, a package in one hand and flowers in the other.

He opened the door before Jerry even had a chance to knock.

"Suppose I hadn't been home?" he said, helping Jerry over the sill.

"I took my chances," Jerry said, smiling gently.

He had a gentle face altogether and a courteous demeanor that did not, however, compromise his tenacity in behalf of his clients. "Well, you seem all right physically, at least. Except for that hopeless look on your face, Simon, you don't look bad at all."

"And you—neat as a pin," Axler said, having himself neither changed his clothes nor shaved for days.

"I brought you flowers. I brought us a box lunch from Dean and DeLuca. Have you had lunch?"

He hadn't even had breakfast, so he merely shrugged and took the gifts and helped Jerry out of his coat.

"You drove up from New York," he said.

"Yes. To see how you're doing and talk to you face-to-face. I have news for you. The Guthrie is doing *Long Day's Journey*. They called to ask about you."

"Why me? I can't act, Jerry, and everyone knows it."

"Nobody knows any such thing. Perhaps people know that you had an emotional setback, but that doesn't set you apart from the human race. They're doing the play next winter. It gets awfully cold out there, but you'd be a wonderful James Tyrone."

"James Tyrone is a lot of lines that you have to say, and I can't say them. James Tyrone is a character that you have to be, and I can't be him. There's no way I can play James Tyrone. I can't play anyone."

"Look, you took a tumble in Washington. That happens to practically everyone sooner or later. There's no ironclad security in any art. People run into an obstacle for reasons no one knows. But the obstacle is a temporary impediment. The obstacle disappears and you go on. There isn't a first-rate actor who hasn't felt discouraged and that his career was over and that he was unable to come out of the bad period he was in. There isn't an actor who hasn't gone up in the middle of a speech and not known where he was. But every time you go out on the stage there's a new chance. Actors can recover their talent. You don't lose the skills if you've been out there for forty years. You still know how to enter and sit down in a chair. John Gielgud used to say that there were times he wished he were like a painter or a writer. Then he could retrieve the bad performance he gave that evening and take it out at midnight and redo it. But he couldn't. He had to do it there. Gielgud went through a very bad time when he could do nothing right. So did Olivier. Olivier went through a terrible period. He had a terrible problem. He couldn't look any of the other actors in the eye. He told the other actors, 'Please don't look at me, because it'll throw me.' For a while he couldn't be alone on the stage. He said to the other actors, 'Don't leave me alone out there.'"

"I know the stories, Jerry. I've heard them all. They don't have to do with me. In the past I never had more than two or three bad nights when I couldn't recover. For two or three nights I would think, 'I know I'm good, I'm just not doing it.' Maybe nobody in the audience knew it, but I knew it—it wasn't there. And on those nights when it isn't there for you it's a labor, I know that, and yet somehow you get by. You can get very good at getting by on what you get by on when you don't have anything else. But that's something different entirely. When I had a truly wretched performance, I would lie awake all night afterward thinking, 'I've lost it, I have no talent, I can't do anything.' Hours would go by, but then all of a sudden, at five or six in the morning, I'd understand what went wrong and I couldn't wait to get to the theater that evening and go on. And I'd go on and I couldn't make a mistake. A beautiful feeling. There are days when you can't wait to get there, when the marriage between you and the role is perfect and there's never a time when you're not happy to sail out onto the stage. Those are important days. And for years I had them one after the other. Well, that's over. Now if I were to go out on the stage, I wouldn't know what I was out there for. Wouldn't know where to begin. In the old days I'd do three hours of preparation in the theater for an eight o'clock curtain. By eight I was deeply inside that role—it was like a trance, like a useful trance. In *The Family Reunion* I was in the theater two and a half hours before the first entrance, working up to how to enter when you are pursued by the Furies. That was hard for me, but I did it."

"You can do it again," Jerry said. "You're forgetting who you are and what you've achieved. Your life has hardly come to nothing. Endlessly you would do things on the stage in a way I never expected, and over the years that was thrilling thousands of times for the audience and always thrilling for me. You went as far away as possible from the obvious thing that any other actor would do. You couldn't be routine. You wanted to go everywhere. Out, out, out, as far out as you could go. And the audience believed in you in every moment, wherever you took them. Sure, nothing is permanently established, but so is nothing permanently lost. Your talent's been mislaid, that's all."

"No, it's gone, Jerry. I can't do any of it again. You're either free or you aren't. You're either free and it's genuine, it's real, it's alive, or it's nothing. I'm not free anymore."

"Okay, let's have some lunch then. And put the flowers in some water. The house looks fine. *You* look fine. A little too slimmed down, I would say, but you still look like yourself. You're eating, I hope."

"I eat."

But when they sat down to lunch in the kitchen, with the flowers in a vase between them, Axler was unable to eat. He saw himself stepping out on the stage to play James Tyrone and the audience bursting into laughter. The anxiety and fear were as naked as that. People would laugh at him because it *was* him.

"What do you do with the days?" Jerry asked.

"Walk. Sleep. Stare into space. Try to read. Try to forget myself for at least one minute of each hour. I watch the news. I'm up to date on the news."

"Who do you see?"

"You."

"This is no way for someone of your accomplishment to live."

"You were kind to come all the way out here, Jerry, but I can't do the play at the Guthrie. I'm finished with all that."

"You're not. You're scared of failing. But that's behind you. You don't realize how one-sided and monomaniacal your perspective has become."

"Did I write the reviews? Did this monomaniac write those reviews? Did I write what they wrote about my Macbeth? I was ludicrous and they said as much. I would just think, 'I got through that line, thank God I got through that line.' I would try to think, 'That wasn't as bad as last night,' when in fact it was worse. Everything I did was false, raucous. I heard this horrible tone in my voice and yet nothing could stop me from fucking up. Hideous. Hideous. I never gave a good performance, not one."

"So you couldn't do Macbeth to your satisfaction. Well, you're not the first. He's a horrible person for an actor to live with. I defy anyone to play him and not be warped by the effort. He's a murderer, he's a killer. Everything is magnified in that play. Frankly, I never understood all that evil. Forget *Macbeth*. Forget those reviews," Jerry said. "It's time to move on. You should come down to New York and begin to work in his studio with Vincent Daniels. You won't be the first whose confidence he's restored. Look, you've done all that tough stuff, Shakespeare, the classics—there's no way this can happen to you with your biography. It's a momentary loss of confidence."

"It isn't a matter of confidence," replied Axler. "I always had a sneaking suspicion that I have no talent whatsoever."

"Well, that's nonsense. That's the depression talking. You hear actors saying it a lot when they're down the way you are. 'I don't have any real talent.

I can memorize the lines. That's about it.' I've heard it a thousand times."

"No, listen to me. When I was fully honest with myself I'd think, 'Okay, all right, I have a modicum of talent or I can at least imitate a talented person.' But it was all a fluke, Jerry, a fluke that a talent was given to me, a fluke that it was taken away. This life's a fluke from start to finish."

"Oh, stop this, Simon. You can still hold attention the way a big star actor does on the stage. You are a titan, for God's sake."

"No, it's a matter of falseness, sheer falseness so pervasive that all I can do is stand on the stage and tell the audience, 'I am a liar. And I can't even lie well. I am a fraud.'"

"And that is more nonsense. Think for a moment of all the bad actors—there are lots of them and they somehow get by. So to tell me that Simon Axler," Jerry said, "with his talent, can't get by is absurd. I've seen you in the past, times when you were not so happy, times when you were in psychic torment in every other way, but put a script in front of you, allow you to access this thing that you do so wonderfully, allow you to become another person, and always it's been liberating for you. Well, that's happened before and it can happen again. The love of what you do well—it can return and it will return. Look, Vincent Daniels is an ace at dealing with problems like yours, a tough, canny, intuitive teacher, highly intelligent, and a scrapper himself."

"I know his name," he told Jerry. "But I've never met him. I never had to meet him."

"He's a maverick, he's a scrapper, and he'll get you back to contending. He'll put the fight back in you. He'll start from scratch if he has to. He'll get you to give up everything you've done before if he must. It'll be a struggle, but in the end he'll get you back to where you should be. I've been to his studio and watched Vincent work. He says, 'Do one moment. We're only dealing with the single moment. Play the moment, play whatever plays for you in that moment, and then go on to the next moment. It doesn't matter where you're going. Don't worry about that. Just take it moment, moment, moment, moment. The job is to be in that moment, with no concern about the rest and no idea where you're going next. Because if you can make one moment work, you can go anywhere.' Now it sounds, I know, like the simplest notion, and that's why it's hard—it's so simple that it's the thing that everybody misses. I believe that Vincent Daniels is the perfect man for you right now. I have complete faith in him for you in your predicament. Here's his card. I came up here to give you this."

Jerry handed him the business card, and so he took it at the same time that he said, "Can't do it."

"What will you do instead? What will you do about all the roles you're ripe to play? It breaks my heart when I think of all those parts you were made for. If you accepted the role of James Tyrone, then you could work with Vincent and find your way through it with him. This is the work he does with actors every day. I can't count the number of times at the Tonys or the Oscars that I heard the winning actor say, 'I want to thank Vincent Daniels.' He is the best."

In response Axler simply shook his head.

"Look," Jerry said, "everyone knows the feeling 'I can't do it,' everyone knows the feeling that they will be revealed to be false—it's every actor's terror. 'They've found me out. I've been found out.' Let's face it, there's a panic that comes with age. I'm that much older than you, and I've been dealing with it for years. One, you get slower. In everything. Even in reading you get slower. If I go fast in reading now, too much of it goes away. My speech is slower, my memory is slower. All these things start to happen. In the process, you start to distrust yourself. You're not as quick as you used to be. And especially if you are an actor. You were a young actor and you memorized scripts one after the other after the other, and you never even thought about it. It was just easy to do. And then all of a sudden it's not as easy, and things don't happen so fast anymore. Memorizing becomes a big anxiety for stage actors going into their sixties and seventies. Once you could memorize a script in a day—now you're lucky to memorize a page in a day. So you start to feel afraid, to feel soft, to feel that you don't have that raw live power anymore. It scares you. With the result, as you say, that you're not free anymore. There's nothing happening—and that's terrifying."

"Jerry, I can't go on with this conversation. We could talk all day, and to no avail. You're good to come and see me and bring me lunch and flowers and to try to help me and encourage me and comfort me and make me feel better. It was tremendously thoughtful. I'm pleased to see you looking well. But the momentum of a life is the momentum of a life. I am now incapable of acting. Something fundamental has vanished. Maybe it had to. Things go. Don't think that my career's been cut short. Think of how long I lasted. When I started out in college I was just fooling around, you know. Acting was a chance to meet girls. Then I took my first theatrical breath. Suddenly I was alive on the stage and breathing like an actor. I started young. I was twenty-two and came to New York for an audition. And I got the part. I began to take classes. Sense-memory exercises. Practice making things real. Before your performance create a reality for yourself to step into. I remember that when I began taking class we'd have a pretend teacup and pretend to drink from it. How hot is it, how full is it, is there a saucer, is there a spoon, are you going to put sugar in it, how many lumps. And then you sip it, and others were transported by this stuff, but I never found any of it helpful. What's more, I couldn't do it. I was no good at the exercises, no good at all. I'd try to do this stuff and it never would work. Everything I did well was coming out of instinct, and doing those exercises and knowing those things were making me look like an actor. I would look ridiculous as I held my pretend teacup and pretended to drink from it. There was always a sly voice inside me saying, 'There is no teacup.' Well, that sly voice has now taken over. No matter how I prepare and what I attempt to do, once I am on the stage there is that sly voice all the time—'There is no teacup.' Jerry, it's over: I can no longer make a play real for people. I can no longer make a role real for myself."

After Jerry had left, Axler went into his study and found his copy of *Long Day's Journey into Night*. He tried to read it but the effort was unbearable. He didn't get beyond page 4—he put Vincent Daniels's card there as a bookmark. At the Kennedy Center it was as though he'd never acted before and now it was as though he'd never read a play before —as though he'd never read *this* play before. The sentences unfolded without meaning. He could not keep straight who was speaking the lines. Sitting there amid his books, he tried to remember plays in which there is a character who commits suicide. Hedda in *Hedda Gabler*, Julie in *Miss Julie*, Phaedra in *Hippolytus*, Jocasta in *Oedipus the King*, almost everyone in *Antigone*, Willy Loman in *Death of a Salesman*, Joe Keller in *All My Sons*, Don Parritt in *The Iceman Cometh*, Simon Stimson in *Our*

Town, Ophelia in *Hamlet*, Othello in *Othello*, Cassius and Brutus in *Julius Caesar*, Goneril in *King Lear*, Antony, Cleopatra, Enobarbus, and Charmian in *Antony and Cleopatra*, the grandfather in *Awake and Sing!*, Ivanov in *Ivanov*, Konstantin in *The Seagull*. And this astonishing list was only of plays in which he had at one time performed. There were more, many more. What was remarkable was the frequency with which suicide enters into drama, as though it were a formula fundamental to the drama, not necessarily supported by the action as dictated by the workings of the genre itself. Deirdre in *Deirdre of the Sorrows*, Hedvig in *The Wild Duck*, Rebecca West in *Rosmersholm*, Christine and Orin in *Mourning Becomes Electra*, both Romeo and Juliet, Sophocles' Ajax. Suicide is a subject dramatists have been contemplating with awe since the fifth century B.C., beguiled by the human beings who are capable of generating emotions that can inspire this most extraordinary act. He should set himself the task of rereading these plays. Yes, everything gruesome must be squarely faced. Nobody should be able to say that he did not think it through.

*

JERRY HAD BROUGHT a manila envelope containing a handful of mail addressed to him in care of the Oppenheim Agency. There was a time when a dozen letters from fans would come to him that way every couple of weeks. Now these few were all that had arrived at Jerry's during the past half year. He sat in the living room idly tearing the envelopes open, reading each letter's first few lines and then balling the page up and throwing it onto the floor. They were all requests for autographed photos—all but one, which took him by surprise and which he read in its entirety.

"I don't know if you'll remember me," the letter began. "I was a patient at Hammerton. I had dinner with you several times. We were in art therapy together. Maybe you won't remember me. I have just finished watching a late-night movie on TV and to my amazement you were in it. You were playing a hardened criminal. It was so startling to see you on the screen, especially in such a menacing role. How different from the man I met! I remember telling you my story. I remember how you listened to me meal after meal. I couldn't stop talking. I was in agony. I thought my life was over. I wanted it to be over. You may not know it but your listening to my story the way you did contributed to my getting through back then. Not that it's been easy. Not that it is now. Not that it ever will be. The monster I was married to has done ineradicable damage to my family. The disaster was worse than I knew when I was hospitalized. Terrible things had been going on for a long time without my knowing anything about them. Tragic things involving my little girl. I remember asking you if you would kill him for me. I told you I would pay. I thought because you were so big you could do it. Mercifully you didn't tell me that I was crazy when I said that but sat there listening to my madness as though I were sane. I thank you for that. But a part of me will never be sane again. It can't be. It couldn't be. It shouldn't be. Stupidly I sentenced the wrong person to death."

The letter went on, a single handwritten paragraph stretching loosely over three more big sheets of paper, and it was signed "Sybil Van Buren." He remembered listening to her story—summoning up his concentration and listening like that to someone other than himself was as close as he had come to acting in a long time and may even have helped *him* to recover. Yes, he remembered her and her story and her asking him to kill her husband, as though he *were* a gangster in a movie rather than another patient in a psychiatric hospital who, big as he was, was as incapable as she of violently ending his own suffering with a gun. People go around killing people in movies all the time, but the reason they make all those movies is that for 99.9 percent of the audience it's impossible to do. And if it's that hard to kill someone else, someone you have every reason to want to destroy, imagine how hard it is to succeed in killing yourself.

2

The Transformation

HE'D KNOWN PEGEEN'S parents as good friends before Pegeen was born and had seen her first in the hospital as a tiny infant nursing at her mother's breast. They'd met when Axler and the newly married Staplefords—he from Michigan, she from Kansas—appeared together in a Greenwich Village church basement production of *Playboy of the Western World*. Axler had played the wonderfully wild lead role of Christy Mahon, the would-be parricide, while the female lead, Pegeen Mike Flaherty, the strong-minded barmaid in her father's pub on the west coast of County Mayo, had been played by Carol Stapleford, then two months pregnant with a first child; Asa Stapleford had played Shawn Keogh, Pegeen's betrothed. When the play's run ended, Axler had been at the closing-night party to cast his vote for Christy as the name for a son and Pegeen Mike as the name for a daughter when the Staplefords' baby arrived.

It was not likely—particularly as Pegeen Mike Stapleford had lived as a lesbian since she was twenty-three—that when she was forty years old and Axler was sixty-five they would become lovers who would speak on the phone every morning upon awakening and would eagerly spend their free time together at his house, where, to his delight, she appropriated two rooms for her own, one of the three bedrooms on the second floor for her things and the downstairs study off the living room for her laptop. There were fireplaces in all the downstairs rooms, even one in the kitchen, and when Pegeen was working in the study, she had a fire going all the time. She lived a little over an hour away, journeying along winding hilly roads that carried her across farm country to his fifty acres of open fields and the large old black-shuttered white farmhouse enclosed by ancient maples and big ashes and long, uneven stone walls. There was nobody but the two of them anywhere nearby. During the first few months they rarely got out of bed before noon. They couldn't leave each other alone.

Yet before her arrival he'd been sure he was finished: finished with acting, with women, with people, finished forever with happiness. He had been in serious physical distress for over a year, barely able to walk any distance or to stand or sit for very long because of the spinal pain that he'd put up with all his adult life but whose debilitating progress had accelerated with age—and so he was sure he was finished with everything. One of his legs would intermittently go dead so that he couldn't raise it properly while walking, and he would miss a step or a curb and fall, opening cuts on his hands and even landing on his face, bloodying his lip or his nose. Only a few months earlier his best and only local friend, an eighty-year-old judge who'd retired some years back, had died of cancer; as a result, though Axler had been based two hours from the city, amid the trees and fields, for thirty years —living there when he wasn't out somewhere in the world performing—he didn't have anyone with whom to talk or to eat a meal, let alone share a bed. And he was thinking again about killing himself as often as he had been before being hospitalized a year earlier. Every morning when he awoke to his emptiness, he determined he couldn't go another day shorn of his skills, alone, workless, and in persistent pain. Once again, the focus was down to suicide; at the center of the dispossession there was only that.

On a frigid gray morning after a week of heavy snowstorms, Axler left the house for the carport to drive the four miles into town and stock up on groceries. Pathways around the house had been kept clear every day by a farmer who did his snowplowing for him, but he walked carefully nonetheless, wearing snow boots with thick treads and carrying a cane and taking tiny steps to prevent himself from slipping and falling. Under his layers of clothes his midsection was enveloped, for safety's sake, in a stiff back brace. As he started out of the house and headed for the carport he spotted a small long-tailed whitish animal standing in the snow between the carport and the barn. It looked at first like a very large rat, and then he realized, from the shape and color of the furless tail and from the snout, that it was a possum about ten inches long. Possums are ordinarily nocturnal, but this one, whose coat looked discolored and scruffy, was down on the snow-covered ground in broad daylight. As Axler approached, the possum waddled feebly off in the direction of the barn and then disappeared into a mound of snow up against the barn's stone foundation. He followed the animal—which was probably sick and nearing its end—and when he got to the mound of snow saw that there was an entry hole cleared at the front. Supporting himself with both hands on his cane, he kneeled down in the snow to peer inside. The possum had retreated too far back into the hole to be seen, but strewn about the front of the cave-like interior was a collection of sticks. He counted them. Six sticks. So that's how it's done, Axler thought. I've got too much. All you need are six.

The following morning while he was making his coffee, he saw the possum through the kitchen window. The animal was standing on its hind legs by the barn, eating snow from a drift, pushing gobs of it into its mouth with its front paws. Hurriedly he put on his boots and his coat, picked up his cane, went out the front door, and came around to the cleared path by the side of the house facing the barn. From some twenty feet away, he called across to the possum in full voice, "How would you like to play James Tyrone? At the Guthrie." The possum just kept eating snow. "You'd be a wonderful James Tyrone!"

After that day, nature's little caricature of him came to an end. He never saw the possum again—either it disappeared or perished—though the snow cave with the six sticks remained intact until the next thaw.

THEN PEGEEN stopped by. She phoned from the little house she'd rented a few miles from Prescott, a small, progressive women's college in western Vermont, where she'd recently taken a teaching job. He lived an hour west, across the state line in rural New York. It was twenty years or more since he'd seen her as a cheerful undergraduate traveling during her vacation with her mother and father. They'd be in his vicinity and stop off for a couple of hours to say hello. Every few years they all got together like that. Asa ran a regional theater in Lansing, Michigan, the town where he'd been born and raised, and Carol acted in the repertory company and taught an acting class at the state university. He'd seen Pegeen on another visit once before, a smiling, shy, sweet-faced kid of ten who'd climbed his trees and swum rapid laps in his pool, a skinny, athletic tomboy who laughed helplessly at all her father's jokes. And before that he'd seen her suckling on the maternity floor of St. Vincent's Hospital in New York.

Now he saw a lithe, full-breasted woman of forty, though with something of the child still in her smile—a smile in which she automatically raised her upper lip to reveal her prominent front teeth—and a lot of the tomboy still in her rocking gait. She was dressed for the countryside, in well-worn work boots and a red zippered jacket, and her hair, which he had incorrectly remembered as blond, like her mother's, was a deep brown and cut close to her skull, so short at the back as to appear clipped by a barber's trimmer. She had the invulnerable air of a happy person, and though her prototype was Rough Gamine, she spoke in an appealingly modulated voice, as if imitating her actress mother's diction.

As he would eventually learn, it had been some time since she'd had what she wanted rather than its grotesque inversion. She'd spent the last two years of a six-year affair suffering in a painfully lonely household in Bozeman, Montana. "The first four years," she told him one night after they'd become lovers, "Priscilla and I had this wonderfully cozy companionship. We used to go camping and hiking all the time, even when it snowed. In the summers we'd go off to places like Alaska and hike and camp up there. It was exciting. We went to New Zealand, we went to Malaysia. There was something childlike about us adventurously roaming around the world together that I loved. We were like two runaways. Then, starting around year five, she slowly drifted away into the computer, and I was left with no one to talk to except the cats. Until then we had done everything side by side. We'd be tucked up in bed, reading—reading to ourselves, reading passages aloud to each other; for such a long time there was the rapturous rapport. Priscilla would never tell people, 'I liked that book,' but rather, 'We liked that book,' or about some place, 'We liked going there,' or about our plans, 'That's what we're going to do this summer.' We. We. We. And then 'we' weren't we—we was over. We was she and her Mac. We was she and her festering secret that blotted out everything else—that she was going to mutilate the body I loved."

The two of them taught at the university in

Bozeman, and during their final two years as a couple, when Priscilla got home from work, she sat in front of her computer until it was time for bed. She spent her weekends in front of the computer. She ate and drank in front of the computer. There was no more talk, no more sex; even hiking and camping in the mountains Pegeen had to undertake on her own or with people other than Priscilla whom she rounded up for companionship. Then one day, six years after they'd met in Montana and pooled their resources and set themselves up as a couple, Priscilla announced that she had begun taking hormonal injections to promote facial hair growth and deepen her voice. Her plan was to have her breasts surgically removed and become a man. Alone, Priscilla admitted, she had been dreaming this up for a long time, and she would not turn back however much Pegeen pleaded. The very next morning Pegeen moved out of the house they jointly owned, taking with her one of the two cats—"Not so great for the cats," said Pegeen, "but that was the least of it"—and she settled into a room at a local motel. She could barely gather enough composure to meet with her classes. Lonely as it had become living with Priscilla, the wound of the betrayal, the nature of the betrayal, was far worse. She cried all the time and began to write letters to colleges hundreds of miles from Montana looking for a new job. She went to a conference where colleges were interviewing people in environmental science and found a position in the East after sleeping with the dean, who became smitten by her and subsequently hired her. The dean was still Pegeen's devoted protector and paramour when Pegeen drove over to pay Axler a visit and determined that after seventeen years as a lesbian she wanted a man—this man, this actor twenty-five years her senior and her family's friend from decades back. If Priscilla could become a heterosexual male, Pegeen could become a heterosexual female.

THAT FIRST AFTERNOON, Axler tripped and fell hard on the wide stone step as he led Pegeen into the house, gashing the meaty side of the hand with which he broke the fall. "Where's your first-aid stuff?" she asked. He told her and she went inside to get it and came back out and cleaned his wound with cotton and peroxide and covered it with a couple of Band-Aids. She'd also brought him a glass of water to drink. Nobody had brought him a glass of water for a long time.

He invited her to stay for dinner. She wound up making it. Nobody had made him dinner for a long time either. She finished off a bottle of beer while he sat at the kitchen table and watched her prepare the meal. There was a chunk of Parmesan cheese in the refrigerator, there were eggs, there was some bacon, there was half a container of cream, and with that and a pound of pasta she made them spaghetti carbonara. He was remembering the sight of her as an infant at her mother's breast while observing her as she worked in his kitchen, behaving as though the place were hers. She was a vibrant presence, solid, fit, brimming with energy, and soon enough he was no longer feeling that he was alone on earth without his talent. He was happy—an unexpected feeling. Usually at the dinner hour he had the worst blues of the day. While she cooked he went into the living room and put on Brendel playing Schubert. He couldn't remember the last time he'd bothered listening to music, and back in the best days of his marriage, it was playing all the time.

"What happened to your wife?" she asked, after they'd eaten the spaghetti and shared a bottle of wine.

"Doesn't matter. Too tedious to discuss."

"How long have you been out here without anyone else?"

"Long enough to be lonelier than I ever thought I could be. It's sometimes astonishing, sitting here month after month, season after season, to think that it's all going on without you. Just as it will when you die."

"What happened to acting?" she asked.

"I don't act anymore."

"That can't be," she said. "What happened?"

"Also too tedious to go into."

"Have you retired or did something happen?"

He stood up and came around the table and she stood and he kissed her.

She smiled with surprise. Laughing, she said, "I'm a sexual anomaly. I sleep with women."

"That wasn't hard to figure out."

Here he kissed her a second time.

"So what are you doing?" she asked.

He shrugged. "I can't say that I know. You've never been with a man?" he asked her.

"When I was in college."

"Are you with a woman now?"

"More or less," she replied. "Are you?"

"No."

He felt the strength in her well-muscled arms, he fumbled with her heavy breasts, he cupped her hard behind in his hands and drew her toward him so that they kissed again. Then he led her to the sofa in the living room, where, blushing furiously as he watched her, she undid her jeans and was with a man for the first time since college. He was with a lesbian for the first time in his life.

Months later he'd say to her, "How come you drove over that afternoon?" "I wanted to see if anybody was with you." "And when you saw?" "I thought, Why not me?" "You calculate like that all the time?" "It isn't calculation. It's pursuing what you want. And," she added, "not pursuing what you no longer want."

THE DEAN who'd hired her and brought her to Prescott was furious when Pegeen told her their affair was over. She was eight years older than Pegeen, earned more than twice as much as Pegeen, had been an important dean for over a decade, and so she refused to believe it or to allow it. She phoned Pegeen to scold her first thing every morning and called her numerous times during the night to shout at her and insult her and demand an explanation. Once she phoned from a local cemetery, where, she announced, she was "stomping around in a fury" because of the way Pegeen had treated her. She accused Pegeen of exploiting her to get the job and then opportunistically dropping her within only weeks of taking it. When Pegeen went to the pool to work out with the swim team twice a week in the late afternoon, the dean turned up to swim at that hour and arranged to take the locker next to Pegeen's. The dean called to invite her to a movie, to a lecture, to a concert and dinner. She called every other day to tell Pegeen that she wanted to see her that coming weekend. Pegeen had already made it clear that she was busy on weekends and didn't want to resume seeing her again. The dean pleaded, she shouted—sometimes she cried. Pegeen was the person she could not live without. A strong, successful, competent woman of forty-eight, a dynamic woman touted to be Prescott's next president, and how easily she could be derailed!

One Sunday afternoon she called his house and asked to speak to Pegeen Stapleford. Axler put down the phone and went into the living room to tell Pegeen the call was for her. "Who is it?" he asked her. Without hesitation, she replied, "Who else could it be? Louise. How does she know where I am? How did she get your number?" He returned to the phone and said, "There's no Pegeen Stapleford here." "Thank you," the caller said and hung up. The next week Pegeen ran into Louise on the campus. Louise told her that she was going away for ten days and that when she came back, Pegeen had "better do something for her" like "make her dinner." Afterward Pegeen was frightened, first because Louise wouldn't leave her alone even after she once again clarified that the affair was over, and second because of the threat Louise's anger embodied. "What's threatened?" he asked. "What? My job. There's no limit to the harm she can do me if she sets her mind to it." "Well, you have me, don't you?" he said. "What does that mean?" "You have me to fall back on. I'm right here."

He was here. She was here. Everyone's possibilities had changed dramatically.

*

THE FIRST ARTICLE of clothing he bought her was a tan close-fitting waist-length leather jacket with a shearling lining that he saw in the window of a shop in the upscale village that lay ten miles through the woods from his house. He went in and purchased what he guessed correctly to be her size. The jacket cost a thousand dollars. She'd never owned anything that expensive before, and she'd never looked so good in anything before. He told her it was for her birthday, whenever that fell. For the next few days, she didn't take it off her back. Then they drove to New York, ostensibly to have some good meals and go to the movies and get away for the weekend together, and he bought her more clothes—by the time the weekend was over, more than five thousand dollars' worth of skirts, blouses, belts, jackets, shoes, and sweaters, outfits in which she looked very different from the way she looked in the clothes she'd brought east with her from Montana. When she'd first showed up at his house, she owned little that couldn't be worn by a sixteen-year-old boy—only now had she begun to give up walking like a sixteen-year-old boy. In the New York stores, after trying on something new in the dressing room, she'd come out to where he was waiting for her to show him how it looked and to hear what he thought. She was paralyzingly self-conscious for only the first few hours; after that she let it happen, eventually emerging coquettishly from the dressing room smiling with delight.

He bought her necklaces, bracelets, and earrings. He bought her luxurious lingerie to replace the sport bras and the gray briefs. He bought her little satin babydolls to replace her flannel pajamas. He bought her calf-high boots, a brown pair and a black pair. The only coat she owned she'd inherited from Priscilla's late mother. It was way too large for her and shaped like a box, and so over the next few months he bought her flattering new coats—five of them. He could have bought her a hundred. He couldn't stop. Living as he did, he rarely spent anything on himself, and nothing made him happier than making her look like she'd never looked before. And in time nothing seemed to make her happier. It was an orgy of spoiling and spending that suited them both just fine.

Still, she didn't want her parents to learn about

the affair. It would cause them too much pain. He thought, More pain than when you told them you were a lesbian? She'd explained to him what had happened on that day back when she was twenty-three. Her mother had cried and said, "I can't imagine anything worse," and her father feigned acceptance but didn't smile again for months. There was a lot of trauma in that home for a long time after Pegeen told them what she was. "Why would learning about me cause them so much pain?" he asked her. "Because they've known you so long. Because you're all the same age." "As you wish," he said. But he couldn't stop pondering her motive. Perhaps she was acting out of the habit of keeping her life in different compartments, the sexual life strictly separated from her life as a daughter; maybe she didn't want the sex contaminated or domesticated by filial concerns. Maybe there was some embarrassment about her turning from sleeping with women to sleeping with a man, and an uncertainty as to whether the switch was going to be permanent. But regardless of what was prompting her, he felt he had made a mistake in allowing her to keep their connection a secret from her family. He was too old not to feel compromised by having to be kept a secret. Nor did he see why a forty-year-old woman should be so concerned about what her parents thought, especially a forty-year-old woman who'd done all sorts of things that her parents disapproved of and whose opposition she weathered. He did not like that she was showing herself to be less than her age, but he didn't push it, not for now, and so her family continued to think she was going along leading her regular life while, with the passing months, she seemed to him, slowly but naturally, to shed the last visible signs of what she now referred to as "my seventeen-year mistake."

Nonetheless, one morning at breakfast, as much to his own surprise as hers, Axler said, "Is this something you really want, Pegeen? Though we've enjoyed each other so far, and the novelty has been strong, and the feeling has been strong, and the pleasure has been strong, I wonder if you know what you're doing."

"Yes, I do. I love this," she said, "and I don't want it to stop."

"But you understand what I'm referring to?"

"Yes. Matters of age. Matters of sexual history.

Your old connection to my parents. Probably twenty things besides. And none of them bother me. Do any of them bother you?"

"Would it perhaps be a good idea," he replied, "before hearts get broken, for us to back off?"

"Aren't you happy?" she asked.

"My life has been very precarious over the past few years. I don't feel the strength that it would take having my hopes dashed. I've had my share of marital misery, and before that my share of breakups with women. It's always painful, it's always harsh, and I don't want to court it at this stage of life."

"Simon, we both have been dropped," she said. "You were at the bottom of a breakdown and your wife picked up and left you to fend for yourself. I was betrayed by Priscilla. Not only did she leave me, she left the body that I'd once loved to become a man with a mustache named Jack. If we do fail let it be because of us, not because of them, not because of your past or mine. I don't want to encourage you in a risk, and I know it is a risk. For both of us, by the way. I feel the risk too. It's of a different sort than yours, of course. But the worst outcome possible is for you to take yourself away from me. I could not bear to lose you now. I will if I have to, but as for the risk—the risk has been taken. We've already done it. It's too late for protection by withdrawing."

"You're saying you don't want to get out of this thing while the getting is good?"

"Absolutely. I want you, you see. I've come to trust that I have you. Don't pull away from me. I love this, and I don't want it to stop. There's nothing else I can say. All I can say is that I'll try if you will. This is no longer just a fling."

"We took the risk," he said, echoing her.

"We took the risk," she replied.

Four words meaning that it would be the worst possible time for her to be dropped by him. She will say whatever she needs to say, he thought, even if the dialogue verges on soap opera, to keep it going because she's still aching, all these months later, from the Priscilla shock and the Louise ultimatums. It's not deception her taking this line—it's the way we are instinctively strategic. But eventually a day will come, Axler thought, when circumstances render her in a much stronger position for it to end, whereas I will have wound up in a weaker position merely from having been too indecisive to cut it off now. And when she is strong and I am weak, the blow that's dealt will be unbearable.

He believed he was seeing clearly into their future, yet he could do nothing to alter the prospect. He was too happy to alter it.

OVER THE MONTHS she had let her hair grow nearly to her shoulders, thick brown hair with a natural sheen that she began to think about having cut in a style unlike the cropped mannish one she'd favored throughout her adult life. One weekend she arrived with a couple of magazines full of photos of different hairstyles, magazines of a kind he'd never seen before. "Where'd you get these?" he asked her. "One of my students," she said. They sat side by side on the sofa in the living room while she turned pages and bent back corners where there was a style pictured that might suit her. Finally they narrowed their preferences down to two, and she tore out those pages and he phoned an actress friend in Manhattan to ask her where Pegeen should go to get her hair cut, the same friend who'd told him where to take Pegeen shopping for clothes and where to go to buy her jewelry. "Wish I had a sugar daddy," the friend said. But he hadn't understood it that way. All he was doing was helping Pegeen to be a woman he would want instead of a woman another woman would want. Together they were absorbed in making this happen.

He went with her to an expensive hairdresser's in the East Sixties. A young Japanese woman cut Pegeen's hair after looking at the two photos they'd brought. He had never seen Pegeen look as disarmed as she did sitting in the chair in front of the mirror after her hair had been washed. He'd never before seen her look so weakened or so at a loss as to how to behave. The sight of her, silent, sheepish, sitting there at the edge of humiliation, unable even to look at her reflection, gave the haircut an entirely transformed meaning, igniting all his self-mistrust and causing him to wonder, as he had more than once, if he wasn't being blinded by a stupendous and desperate illusion. What is the draw of a woman like this to a man who is losing so much? Wasn't he making her pretend to be someone other than who she was? Wasn't he dressing her up in costume as though a costly skirt could dispose of nearly two decades of lived experience? Wasn't he distorting her while telling himself a lie—and a lie that in the end might be anything but harmless? What if he proved to be no more than a brief male intrusion into a lesbian life?

But then Pegeen's thick brown shiny hair was cut —cut to below the base of her neck in a choppy way so none of the layers were even, a look that gave her precisely the right cared-for devil-may-care air of slight dishevelment—and she seemed so transformed that all these unanswered questions ceased to trouble him; they did not even require serious thought. It took her a little longer than it took him to be convinced that the two of them had chosen correctly, but in only a few days the haircut and all it signified about her allowing him to shape her, to determine what she should look like and advance an idea of what her true life was, appeared to have become more than just acceptable. Perhaps because she looked so great in his eyes she did not bridle at continuing to submit to his ministrations, alien though that might have been to a lifelong sense of herself. If indeed hers was the will that was submitting—if indeed it wasn't she who had taken him over completely, taken him up and taken him over.

*

LATE ONE FRIDAY AFTERNOON Pegeen arrived at his house in distress—out in Lansing her family had received a midnight phone call from Louise to tell them how she had been opportunistically exploited and deceived by their daughter.

"What else?" he said.

His question brought Pegeen close to tears. "She told them about you. She said I was living with you."

"And what did they say to that?"

"My mother was the one who answered. He was asleep."

"And how did she take it?"

"She asked me if it was true. I told her I wasn't living with you. I told her we had become close friends."

"What did your father say?"

"He never came to the phone."

"Why didn't he?"

"I don't know. That miserable bitch! Why won't she stop!" she cried. "That obsessive, possessive, jealous, rancorous bitch!"

"Does it really matter to you that she told your parents?"

"Doesn't it matter to you?" Pegeen asked him.

"Only inasmuch as it troubles you. Otherwise not at all. I think it's all to the good."

"What do I say when I talk to my father?" she asked.

"Pegeen Mike—say whatever you like."

"Suppose he decides not to talk to me at all."

"I doubt that will happen."

"Suppose he wants to talk to you."

"Then he and I will talk," Axler said.

"How angry is he?"

"Your father is a reasonable and sensible man. Why would he be angry?"

"Oh, that bitch—she is completely whacked. She's out of control."

"Yes," he said, "the thought of you tortures her. But you're not out of control, I'm not, and neither are your mother and father."

"Then why didn't my father speak to me?"

"If you're so worried, call and ask him. Perhaps you'd like me to speak to him."

"No, I'll do it—I'll do it myself."

She waited until after they'd eaten before phoning Lansing, and then doing it from her study, behind the closed door. After fifteen minutes she came out carrying the phone and pointed with it toward him.

Axler took the phone. "Asa? Hello."

"Hi there. I hear you seduced my daughter."

"I'm having an affair with her, that is true."

"Well, I can't say I'm not a little astonished."

"Well," Axler replied with a laugh, "I can't say that I'm not either."

"When she told me she was going to visit you, I really never figured that this was in the cards," Asa said.

"Well, I'm glad you're all right with it," Axler replied.

There was a pause before Asa answered, "Pegeen's a free agent. She left her childhood long ago. Look, Carol wants to say hello," Asa said and then passed the phone to his wife.

"Well, well," Carol said, "who ever could have imagined this when we were all kiddies in New York?"

"No one," Axler replied. "I couldn't have imagined it the day she showed up here."

"Is my daughter doing the right thing?" Carol asked him.

"I think so."

"What is your plan?" Carol asked.

"I have no plan."

"Pegeen has always surprised us."

"She surprised me too," Axler said. "I think she's no less surprised."

"Well, she surprised her friend Louise."

He did not bother to reply that Louise was something of a surprise herself. Carol's intention, clearly, was to be mild and friendly, but he was sure from the brittleness of her tone that the call was an ordeal and that she and Asa were simply doing the right thing, which was their way, doing the sensible thing that would make Pegeen happiest. They did not want to alienate her at forty as they had at twenty-three when she'd told them she was a lesbian.

IN FACT, CAROL FLEW in from Michigan the following Saturday to meet Pegeen in New York for lunch. Pegeen drove down to the city that morning and got back about eight that night. He had made dinner for them, and only when dinner was over did he ask her how it had gone.

"Well, what did she say?" Axler asked.

"Do you want me to be entirely honest?" Pegeen replied.

"Please," he said.

"All right," she said, "I'll try to remember as exactly as I can. It was kind of the benign third degree. There was nothing vulgar or self-serving about her. Just Mother's flat-out Kansas candor."

"Go ahead."

"You want to know everything," Pegeen said.

"Yes," he replied.

"Well, first off, at the restaurant, she breezed right by my table—she failed to recognize me. I said, 'Mother,' and then she turned back and she said, 'Oh, my goodness, it's my daughter. Don't you look pretty.' And I said, 'Pretty? Didn't you think I was pretty before?' And she said, 'A new hairdo, clothes of a kind I never saw you wear before.' And I said, 'More feminine, you mean.' 'Decidedly,' she said, 'yes. It's very flattering, dear. How long has this been going on?' I told her, and she said, 'That's a very nice haircut. It couldn't have been inexpensive.' And I said to her, 'I'm just trying something new.' And she said, 'I guess you are trying something new, in many ways. I came out because I want to be sure that you have thought through all the implications of your affair.' I told her that I wasn't sure anyone ever thinks through being with someone romantically. I told her that it made me very happy right now. And so she said, 'News reached us that he was in a psychiatric hospital. Some people say he was there six months, some say a year— I don't really know the facts.' I told her that you were there for twenty-six days a full twelve months ago and that it had to do with performance problems on the stage. I said that you temporarily lost your power to act, and separated from your acting, you came apart. I said that whatever emotional or mental problems you had then, they didn't manifest themselves in our life together now. I said you were as sane or saner than anyone I've ever been with, and that when we're together you seem stable and quite happy. And she asked, 'Is he still in the same bind with his acting?' And I said yes and no—you were, but I thought that as a result of meeting me and being with me, it was no longer the same tragedy it had been. It was now more like an athlete who's been injured and sidelined and is waiting to heal. And she said, 'You don't feel you have to rescue him, do you?' I assured her that I did not, and she asked how you filled your time, and I said, 'He sees me. I think he plans to continue seeing me. He reads. He buys me clothes.' Well, she leaped on that—'So these are clothes he bought for you. Well, I would think there might be a certain rescue fantasy working there.' I told her that she was making too much of it and that it was just fun for both of us, and why couldn't we leave it at that? I said, 'He's not trying to influence me in any way I don't want to be influenced.' She asked, 'Do you go with him when he buys you clothes?' And I said, 'Usually. But again, I think it makes him happy. And I can see that in him. Since it happens to be an experiment I want to conduct as well,' I told her, 'I don't see why anyone should be concerned.' And that's when the tenor of the conversation changed. She said, 'Well, I have to tell you that I am concerned. You're new to the world of men, and it strikes me as strange—or maybe not so strange—that the man you should choose to initiate this new life with is a man twenty-five years older than you are who has been through a breakdown that led to his being institutionalized. And who now is essentially unemployed. All those things don't bode well to me.' I told her that it didn't seem any worse than the situation I was in before, with someone whom I

once loved very much and who told me one morning, 'I can't go on in this body,' and decided she
wanted to be a man. And then I made my speech,
the speech I'd prepared and recited aloud driving
down. I said, 'As for his age, Mother, I don't see it
as a problem. If I'm going to try to be attractive to
men and also learn whether I am attracted to men,
this seems to be the best measure of it. This person
is the test. The twenty-five years register with me
as twenty-five years more experience than someone
would have if I were trying this with a man my own
age. We're not talking about getting married. I told
you—we're just enjoying each other. I'm enjoying
him, in part, because he is twenty-five years older.'
And she said, 'And he's enjoying you because you're
twenty-five years younger.' I said, 'Don't be of-
fended, Mother, but are you at all jealous?' And she
laughed and said, 'Dear, I'm sixty-three and happily
married to your father for over forty years. It's
true,' she said, 'and you may get a kick out of knowing this, but when I played Pegeen Mike and Simon
played Christy in the Synge play, I had a crush on
him. Who didn't? He was wildly attractive, ener-
getic, exuberant, playful, he was a big forceful actor,
a wonderful actor, already his talent obviously a

huge cut above everyone else's. So, yes, I had a crush, but I was already married and pregnant with you. The crush was something I passed through. I think I've seen him no more than ten times in the intervening years. I respect him enormously as an actor. But I continue to be concerned by that hospital stay. It's no small thing for someone to commit himself to a psychiatric hospital and to be there for however long or short a period it was. Look,' she said, 'for me the important thing is that you're not going into this blind. You don't want to be doing something that, for lack of experience, a twenty-year-old might do. I don't want you to act out of innocence.' And I said, 'I'm hardly innocent, Mother.' I asked her what she was afraid might happen that couldn't happen with anyone. And she said, 'What am I afraid of? I'm afraid of the fact that he is growing older by the day. That's the way it works. You're sixty-five and then you're sixty-six and then you're sixty-seven, and so on. In a few years he'll be seventy. You'll be with a seventy-year-old man. And it won't stop there,' she told me. 'After that he'll become a seventy-five-year-old man. It never stops. It goes on. He'll begin to have health problems such as the elderly have, and maybe things even worse, and you're going to be the person responsible for his care. Are you in love with him?' she said. I said I thought that I was. And she asked, 'Is he in love with you?' And I said I thought that you were. I said, 'I think it'll be fine, Mother. It has occurred to me that he has to worry more than I do. That this is a more precarious situation for him than it is for me.' She asked, 'How so?' I said, 'Well, as you say, I'm trying this for the first time. Although it's a novelty for him as well, it's not nearly as much of one as it is for me. I've been very surprised by how much I've enjoyed it. But I couldn't yet declare that it's definitely the permutation I will always want.' And she said, 'Well, all right, I don't want to go on and on and give this an urgency it doesn't have and may never have. I just thought it was important for me to see you, and I must say, once again, I'm very impressed by your appearance.' And I asked her, 'Does it make you think you would still have preferred a daughter who was straight?' She said, 'It makes me think that you would prefer not to be a lesbian any longer. You can, of course, do whatever you like. In your independent youth you educated *us* about that. But I can't fail to notice the physical change. You've taken great care that everybody *should* notice that. You even do your eyes. It's an impressive transformation.' That's when I said, 'What do you think Dad would think?' And she said, 'He couldn't be here because a new play opens in a few days and he can't leave it. But he wanted to come to see you, and as soon as the play is on, he will come, if that's all right with you. And then you can ask him directly what he thinks. So there we are. Want to go shopping?' she said to me. 'I'm admiring your shoes. Where'd you get them?' I told her, and she said, 'Would you object if I bought a pair like that? Want to go with me to get them?' And so we took a taxi to Madison Avenue and she bought a pair of two-toned pink-and-beige patent leather pumps with a pointy toe and a kitten heel in her size. Now she's walking around Michigan in my Prada shoes. She also admired my skirt, so we went shopping for a skirt for her cut like mine down in SoHo. Good ending, isn't it? But late in the afternoon, you know what she said, before leaving for the airport with her bags from the shopping? This, and not the shoes, is the true ending. She said, 'What you were trying to do with me at lunch, Pegeen, was make it sound like the sanest and most reasonable arrangement on the planet, when of course it isn't. But people on the outside are only going to frustrate you if they try to talk you out of what you wake up every day wanting and what is buoying you above everybody's humdrum sameness. I have to tell you that when I first learned of this I thought it was wacky and ill advised. And now that I've spoken with you and spent the day with you and been shopping with you for the first time, really, since you went off to college, now that I've seen that you're completely calm, rational, and thoughtful about it, I still think it's wacky and ill advised.'"

Here Pegeen stopped. It had taken her close to half an hour to repeat the conversation to him, and in that time he had not spoken or moved from his chair, nor had he told her to stop on any of those several occasions when he thought he'd heard enough. But it was not in his interest to tell her to stop—it was in his interest to find out everything, to hear everything, even, if he had to, to hear her say, "I couldn't yet declare that it's definitely the permutation I will always want."

"That's it. That's all," Pegeen said. "That's pretty close to what was said."

"Was it better or worse than you expected?" he asked.

"Much better. I was very anxious driving down there."

"Well, it sounds as though you had no need to be. You handled yourself very well."

"Then I was very anxious coming back, about telling you all this and knowing that, if I was truthful, you weren't going to like everything you heard."

"Well, there was no need for that either."

"Really? I hope my telling you everything hasn't turned you against my mother."

"Your mother said what a mother would say. I understand." He laughed and said, "I can't say that I disagree with her."

Softly, and flushing as she spoke, Pegeen said, "I hope it hasn't turned you against me."

"It's made me admire you," he said. "You didn't flinch from anything, either in talking with her or now in talking with me."

"Truly? You're not hurt?"

"No." But of course he was—hurt and angry. He had sat there listening quietly—intently listening as he'd been listening all his life, offstage and on—but he was particularly stung by Carol's clarification of the aging process and the jeopardy in which it placed her daughter. Nor, however softly he now spoke, was he unperturbed by "wacky and ill advised." The whole thing disgusted him, really. It might be all right if Pegeen were twenty-two and there were forty years' difference between them, but why this peculiar proprietary relationship with an adventurous forty-year-old? And what the hell did a woman of forty care what her parents wanted? A part of them, he thought, should be happy that she was with him, if only from a venal point of view. Here is this eminent man with a lot of money who's going to take care of her. After all, she's not getting any younger herself. She settles down with someone who's achieved something in life— what's so wrong with that? Instead the message is: Don't set yourself up to be caretaker of a crazy old guy.

However, since Pegeen had seemingly rejected Carol's account of him, he thought it best to stay silent about that as well as everything else that he didn't like. What would be the good of attacking her mother for butting in? Better to appear to laugh it off. If she should come to see him through her mother's eyes, there was nothing he could say or do to stop her anyway.

"You're wonderful to me," Pegeen said to him. "You're what the doctor ordered."

"And you to me," he said, and he left it at that. He didn't go on from there to add, "As for your parents, I'd just as soon spare them, but I can't arrange my life according to their feelings. Their feelings don't matter that much to me, frankly, and at this stage of the game they really shouldn't matter that much to you either." No, he would not take off in that direction. Instead he would sit tight and be patient and hope the family would fade away.

The next day Pegeen devoted to stripping the wallpaper in her study. The wallpaper had been chosen by Victoria many years before, and though Axler didn't care about it one way or another, Pegeen couldn't stand the look of it and asked if she could take it down. He told her the room was hers to do with as she liked, as was the upstairs back bedroom and the bathroom beside it, as indeed was every room in the house. He told her he could easily get a painter in to do the job, but she insisted on stripping the walls and painting them herself, thereby making the study officially hers. She had all the necessary tools for stripping wallpaper at her house, and she had brought them with her to begin the job that Sunday, the very day after her mother, down in New York, had questioned the wisdom of her being there at all. He must have gone in to watch her removing the wallpaper ten times during the course of the day, and each time came away with the same reassuring thought: she wouldn't be working away like that if Carol had succeeded in persuading her to leave him. She wouldn't be doing what she was doing if she weren't planning to stay.

That evening Pegeen drove back to the college, where she had a class to teach early the following morning. When the phone rang around ten on Sunday night he thought it was she who was calling to say that she was safely home. It wasn't. It was the jilted dean. "Be forewarned, Mr. Famous: she's desirable, she's audacious, and she's utterly ruthless, utterly cold-hearted, incomparably selfish, and completely amoral." And with that, the dean hung up.

THE NEXT MORNING Axler dropped off his car to be serviced, and the mechanic gave him a ride back

home in his tow truck. He would return the car to
Axler at the end of the day when the job was done.
Around noon, when Axler went into the kitchen to
make a sandwich for himself, he happened to look
out the window and saw something dart across the
field adjacent to the barn and then disappear behind it. It was a person this time, not a possum. He
stood back from the kitchen window and waited
to see if perhaps there was a second, third, or
fourth person lurking anywhere else. There had
been a worrisome series of break-ins throughout
the county in recent months, mainly into unoccu-
pied houses owned by weekenders, and he wondered if the absence of a car in his carport had
caught the attention of the robbers and made him a
target for a daytime theft. Quickly, he headed for
the attic to get his shotgun and load it with shells.
Then he went back downstairs to survey his prop-
erty from the kitchen window. A hundred yards to
the north, on the road that ran perpendicular to his,
he could see a parked car, but it was too far for him
to make out whether there was anyone inside it. It
was unusual to see a car parked there at any time of
the day or night—there was a thickly wooded hill
on the far side of the road, and on his side, open

fields leading up to his barn, carport, and house. Suddenly the person hiding back of the barn came sneaking along the side of the barn and made a rush for the front of the house. From the kitchen he saw that the intruder was a tall, thin, redheaded woman dressed in jeans and a navy blue ski jacket. She was peering into the living room through a front window. As he was still uncertain whether or not she was alone, for the moment he froze, the gun in his hands. Soon she began to move from one window to the next, stopping each time to get a good look at the room inside. He slipped out of the house through the back door and, without her seeing him, came to within ten feet of where she was staring into one of the living room windows on the south side of the house.

Aiming the rifle at her, he spoke. "What can I do for you, lady?"

"Oh!" she cried when she turned and saw him. "Oh, I'm sorry."

"Are you alone?"

"Yes. I'm alone. I'm Louise Renner."

"You're the dean."

"Yes."

She did not look much older than Pegeen, but

she was a good deal taller, only inches shorter than he was, and what with her erect carriage and the red hair pulled away from her high forehead and knotted severely at the back of her neck, there was a heroically statuesque aura to this woman. "What do you think you're doing?" he asked her.

"I'm trespassing, I know. I intended no harm. I thought no one was home."

"Have you been here before?"

"Only to drive by."

"Why?"

"Could you lower that gun? It's making me very nervous."

"Well, you made me nervous, peeking into my windows."

"I'm sorry. I apologize. I've been stupid. This is shameful. I'll go."

"What were you up to?"

"You know what I was up to," she said.

"You tell me."

"I only wanted to see where she goes every weekend."

"You're in a bad way. You drove from Vermont to find that out."

"She promised we'd be together forever, and

three weeks later she left. I apologize again. This has never happened to me before. I should never have come here."

"And it probably doesn't help much, your meeting me."

"It doesn't."

"It makes you boil with jealousy," he said.

"With hatred, if you want the truth."

"It's you who phoned last night."

"I'm not completely in charge of myself," she replied.

"You're obsessed, so you phone, you're obsessed, so you stalk. You're a very attractive woman nonetheless."

"I've never been told that before by a man with a gun."

"I don't know why she left you for me," he said.

"Oh, don't you?"

"You're a red-haired Valkyrie and I'm an old man."

"An old man who's a star, Mr. Axler. Don't pretend to be no one."

"Would you like to come inside?" he asked.

"Why? Do you want to seduce me too? Is that your specialty, retooling lesbians?"

"Madam, it isn't I who was the Peeping Tom. It isn't I who phoned her parents in Michigan at midnight. It isn't I who anonymously phoned 'Mr. Famous' last night. No need to take the accusatory tone so quickly."

"I'm not myself."

"Do you think she's worth it?"

"No. Of course not," she said. "She's not at all beautiful. She's not that intelligent. And she's not that grown up. She's an unusually childish person for her age. She's a kid, really. She turned her Montana lover into a man. She's turned me into a beggar. Who knows what she's turning you into. She leaves a trail of disaster. Where does the power come from?"

"Take a guess," he said.

"Is it that that makes for disaster?" the dean asked.

"Something about her sexually is very potent," he said, and saw her cringe at the words. But then it could not be easy for the loser to stand there and confront the person who had won.

"There's plenty that's potent," the dean said. "She's a girl-boy. She's a child-adult. There's an adolescent in her that's not grown up. She's a cunning naif. But it's not her sexuality on its own that does it—it's us. It's we who endow her with the power to wreck. Pegeen's nobody, you know."

"You wouldn't be suffering so if she were nobody. She wouldn't be here if she were nobody. Look, you might as well step inside. Then you can see everything up close." And he could hear more about Pegeen, seared though her observations would be by Pegeen's having "exploited" her. Yes, he wanted to hear her speak out of the depths of her wound about the closest person on earth to him.

"This has been more than enough," the dean said.

"Come inside," he said.

"No."

"Are you afraid of me?" he asked.

"I've done something foolish for which I apologize. I've trespassed and I'm sorry. And now I'd like you to let me go."

"I'm not holding you. You have a way of trying to turn the moral tables on me. But I didn't invite you here in the first place."

"Then why do you want me to come inside? Because of the triumph it would be to sleep with the woman that Pegeen used to sleep with?"

"I have no such ambition. I'm satisfied with things as they are. I was being polite. I could offer you a cup of coffee."

"No," the dean said coldly. "No, you want to fuck me."

"Is that what you want me to want?"

"That is what you want."

"Is that what you came here to try to get me to do? So as to pay Pegeen back in kind?"

All at once she could conceal her misery no longer and burst into tears. "Too late, too late," she sobbed.

He did not understand what she was referring to, but he didn't ask. She cried with her face buried in her hands while he turned and, with the gun at his side, went back into the house through the rear door, trying to believe that nothing Louise had said about Pegeen, either there outside the house or the night before on the phone, could possibly be taken seriously.

When he called Pegeen that night he made no reference to what had happened that afternoon nor did he tell Pegeen about Louise's visit when she came for the weekend, nor, while they were having sex, was he able to keep the red-haired Valkyrie out of his mind and the fantasy of what hadn't happened.

3

The Last Act

THE PAIN FROM the spinal condition made it impossible for him to fuck her from above or even from the side, and so he lay on his back and she mounted him, supporting herself on her knees and her hands so as not to lower her weight onto his pelvis. At first she lost all her know-how up there and he had to guide her with his two hands to give her the idea. "I don't know what to do," Pegeen said shyly. "You're on a horse," Axler told her. "Ride it." When he worked his thumb into her ass she sighed with pleasure and whispered, "Nobody's ever put anything in there before"—"Unlikely," he whispered back—and when later he put his cock in there, she took as much as she could of it until she couldn't take any more. "Did it hurt?" he asked her. "It hurt, but it's you." Often she would hold his cock

in her palm afterward and stare as the erection sub-
sided. "What are you contemplating?" he asked. "It
fills you up," she said, "the way dildos and fingers
don't. It's alive. It's a living thing." She quickly mas-
tered riding the horse, and soon while she worked
slowly up and down she began to say, "Hit me," and
when he hit her, she said mockingly, "Is that as
hard as you can do it?" "Your face is already red."
"Harder," she said. "Okay, but why?" "Because I've
given you permission to do it. Because it hurts. Because it makes me feel like a little girl and it makes
me feel like a whore. Go ahead. Harder."

She had a small plastic bag of sex toys that she
brought with her one weekend, and she spilled
them out on the sheets when they were getting
ready for bed. He'd seen his share of dildos, but
never, other than in pictures, the strap-on leather
harness that held the dildo secure and enabled
one woman to mount and penetrate another. He'd
asked her to bring her toys with her, and now he
watched as she pulled the harness over her thighs
and on up to her hips, where she tightened it like a
belt. She looked like a gunslinger getting dressed,
a gunslinger with a swagger. Then she inserted a
green rubber dildo into a slot in the harness that

was just about level with her clitoris. She stood alongside the bed wearing only that. "Let me see yours," she said. He removed his pants and threw them over the side of the bed while she grabbed the green cock and, having lubricated it first with baby oil, pretended to masturbate like a man. Admiringly he said, "It looks authentic." "You want me to fuck you with it." "No, thanks," he said. "I wouldn't hurt you," she said cajolingly, kittenishly lowering her voice. "I promise to be very gentle with you," she said. "Funny, but you don't look like you'll be gentle." "You mustn't be deceived by appearances. Oh, let me," she said, laughing, "you'll *like* it. It's a new frontier." "*You'll* like it. No, I'd prefer you to suck me off," he said. "While I wear my cock," she said. "Yes." "While I wear my big thick green cock." "That's what I want." "While I wear my big green cock and you play with my tits." "That sounds right." "And after I suck you off," she said, "you'll suck me off. You'll go down on my big green cock." "I could do that," he said. "So—that you could do. You draw strange boundaries. In any event, you should know you're still a very twisted man to be turned on by a girl like me." "I may well be a twisted man, but I don't believe you qualify as a girl like you any longer." "Oh, don't you now?" "Not with that two-hundred-dollar haircut. Not with those clothes. Not with your own mother following your fashion in footwear." Her hand continued slowly pumping the dildo. "You really think you've fucked the lesbian out of me in ten months?" "Are you telling me that you're still sleeping with women?" he asked. She just kept pumping the dildo. "Are you, Pegeen?" With her free hand she held up two fingers. "What does that mean?" he asked. "Twice." "With Louise?" "Don't be crazy." "With whom, then?" She flushed. "Two teams of girls were playing softball on the field I drive by on the way to school. I parked the car and I got out and went over and stood by the bench." After a pause, she confessed, "When the game was over the pitcher with the blond ponytail came to the house with me." "And the second time?" "The other pitcher with the blond ponytail." "That leaves quite a few players waiting their turn," he said. "I didn't intend to do it," she said, still stroking the green cock. "Perhaps, Pegeen Mike," he said, falling into the Irish accent he hadn't used since acting in *Playboy*, "you should tell me if you have plans to do it again. I'd rather you wouldn't," he said, knowing himself helpless to hold on to her and keep her his alone, knowing that his ardor had been laughable—and trying to hide his feelings behind the brogue. "I told you, I wasn't planning to do it at all," and then, either because desire had overpowered her or because she wanted to shut him up, she lowered her lips down the length of his cock while his gaze remained hypnotically fastened to hers, and the helplessness in him, the knowledge that the affair was a futile folly and that Pegeen's history was unmalleable and Pegeen unattainable and that he was bringing a new misfortune down on his head, began to abate. The oddity of this combination would have put off many people. Only the oddity was what was so exciting. But the terror remained too, the terror of going back to being completely finished. The terror of becoming the next Louise, the reproachful, crazed, avenging ex.

PEGEEN'S FATHER hadn't helped things any when he had come to see her in New York on the Saturday following her mother's visit. Asa picked up where Carol had left off in citing the dangers of their liaison, moving from her lover's perilous age to his perilous psychiatric condition. Axler's strategy remained the same, however: tolerate whatever you hear; don't rush to challenge the parents so long as Pegeen doesn't yield.

"Your mother was right—that's a wonderful haircut," she'd reported her father's telling her. "And she was right about your clothes too," he'd said. "Yes? Do you think I look nice?" "You look terrific," he'd said. "Better than I used to?" "Different. Quite different." "Do I look more like the daughter you would have liked to have had?" "You certainly have an air you never had before. Now tell me about Simon." "After the hard time he had at the Kennedy Center," she'd said, "he wound up at a psychiatric hospital. Is that what you want to talk about?" she'd asked. "Yes, it is," he'd said. "We all have serious problems, Dad." "We all have serious problems but we don't all wind up in psychiatric hospitals." "While we're at it," she'd said, "what about the difference in age? Don't you want to ask about that?" "Let me ask you something else: are you starstruck, Pegeen? You know how certain kinds of characters carry around their force field, an encircling electric force field? It comes, in his case, with being a star. Are you starstruck?" She'd laughed. "At the beginning, probably. By this time,

I assure you, he's just himself." "May I ask how committed you are to each other?" he'd said. "We don't really talk about it." "Maybe you ought to talk about it with me then. Are you going to marry him, Pegeen?" "I don't think he's interested in marrying anyone." "Are you?" "Why are you treating me as though I'm twelve?" she'd said. "Because it may be that where men are concerned you are more twelve than forty. Look, Simon Axler's an intriguing actor, and probably to a woman an intriguing man. But he is the age he is, and you are the age you are. He has had the life he's had, with its triumphant ups and its cataclysmic downs, and you have had the life you have had. And because those downs of his worry me greatly, I'm not going to talk about them as glibly as you do. I'm not going to tell you that I'm not going to try to bring any pressure to bear on you. I am going to do just that."

And that he did—unlike the mother, he didn't end the day shopping with his daughter but instead he phoned her at her house every night around dinnertime to continue, in much the same strong vein, the conversation that had begun at lunch in New York. Rarely did father and daughter speak for less than an hour.

In bed, the evening after she'd seen her father in New York, Axler had said to her, "I want you to know, Pegeen, that I'm flabbergasted by all this stuff with your parents. I don't understand the place they are coming to play in our lives. It seems entirely too large and, all things considered, a little absurd. On the other hand, I recognize that at any stage of life there are mysteries about people and their attachments to their parents that can be surprising. This being so, let me make a proposal: if you want me to fly out to Michigan and talk to your father, I'll fly out to Michigan, and I'll sit and listen to every word he wants to say, and when he tells me why he's against this, I won't even argue—I'll side with him. I'll tell him that everything he's concerned about makes perfect sense and that I agree —it is an unlikely arrangement on the face of it, and there are, to be sure, risks involved. But the fact remains that his daughter and I feel as we do about each other. And the fact that he and Carol and I were friends as youngsters back in New York is of no relevance whatsoever. That's the only defense I will make, Pegeen, if you want me to go and see him. It's up to you. I'll do it this week if you want me to. I'll do it tomorrow if that's what you want."

"His seeing me was quite enough," she replied. "There's no need for this to be carried further. Especially as you have made it clear that you think it's already been carried too far."

"I'm not so sure you're right," he said. "Better to take on the raging father—"

"But my father isn't raging, it isn't in his nature to rage, and I don't think there's any need to provoke a scene when there isn't a scene in the offing."

He thought, Oh, there's a scene in the offing all right—the two upstanding squares you have for parents are not through. But he only said to her, "Okay. I simply wanted to make the offer. It's finally up to you."

But was that so? Wasn't it up to him to neutralize them by opposing them rather than by simply leaving things to turn out opportunely on their own? He should, in fact, have accompanied her to New York—he should have insisted on being there and facing Asa down. Despite what Pegeen had said to assure him, he was reluctant to give up the idea that Asa was a father in a rage whom he should confront rather than flee. *Are you starstruck?* Of course that's what he would believe, he who never got the big roles. Yes, thought Axler, that my fame stole away his only daughter, the fame that Asa himself could never garner.

It was in the middle of the next week that he got around to reading the previous Friday's county newspaper and the front-page story about a murder that had taken place in a well-to-do suburban town some twenty-five miles away. A man in his forties, a successful plastic surgeon, had been shot dead by his estranged wife. The wife was Sybil Van Buren.

The two were apparently living apart by then. She had driven to his house across town from hers, and as soon as he opened the door had shot him twice in the chest, killing him instantly. She had dropped the murder weapon on the doorstep, then gone back and sat in her parked car until the police came and took her to the station to be booked. When she had left home that morning, she had already arranged for the babysitter to spend the day with the two children.

Axler phoned Pegeen and told her what had happened.

"Did you think she could have done this?" Pegeen asked.

"Such a helpless person? No. Never. She had the motive—the molestation—but homicide? She asked if I would murder him for her. She said, 'I need someone to kill this evil man.'"

"What a shocking story," Pegeen said.

"This fragile-looking woman built on the frailest, childlike scale. The least menacing person one could encounter."

"They'll never convict her," Pegeen said.

"Maybe they will, maybe they won't. Maybe she'll plead temporary insanity and get off. But what will become of her then? What will become of the child? If the little girl wasn't already doomed because of what the stepfather did, now she's doomed because of what her mother's done. Not to mention their little boy."

"Would you like me to come tonight? You sound shaky."

"No, no," he said. "I'm all right. I've just never known anyone who's killed somebody off the stage."

"I'm going to come over later," Pegeen said.

And when she did, they sat in the living room after dinner and he repeated to her in detail everything he remembered Sybil Van Buren saying to him at the hospital. He found her letter—the letter that had been mailed to him in care of Jerry's office—and gave it to Pegeen to read.

"The husband claimed to be innocent," Axler explained. "He claimed she was seeing things."

"Was she?"

"I didn't think so. I saw her suffering. I believed her story."

During the day, he had read the article again and again and repeatedly looked at the photograph of Sybil that the paper had published, a studio portrait in which she looked less like a married woman in her thirties, let alone a Clytemnestra, than like a high school cheerleader, someone who as yet had been through nothing in life.

The following day he phoned Information and, easy as that, got the Van Burens' phone number. When he called, a woman answered who identified herself as Sybil's sister. He told her who he was and told her about Sybil's letter. He read it to her over the phone. They agreed she would pass it on to Sybil's lawyer.

"Are you able to see her?" he asked.

"Only with the lawyer. She gets teary about not

seeing the children. Otherwise she's unnervingly calm."

"Does she talk about the murder?"

"She says, 'It had to be done.' You'd think it was her fiftieth, not her first. She's in a very strange state. The gravity seems to escape her. It's as though the gravity is all behind her."

"For the moment," he said.

"I've been thinking the same. There's a great crash going to occur. She won't be living behind this placid mask for long. There must be a suicide watch on her cell. I'm frightened of what's coming next."

"Of course. What she did in no way jibes with the woman I knew. Why did she do this after all this time?"

"Because even when John moved out, he continued to deny everything and to tell her that she was delusional, and that put her into a mad frenzy. On the morning that she was going to see him, she told me that by whatever means it took she was going to extract a confession from him. I said, 'Don't see him. It will only drive you over the edge.' And I was right. I was the one who had wanted her to go to the district attorney and bring charges. I was the one who told her that she should have him put behind bars. But she refused: he wasn't a nobody and the case would wind up in the papers and on TV and Alison would get dragged into a courtroom nightmare to be exposed to yet more horror. Her saying this is why I never dreamed that extracting a confession 'by any means' would involve the use of his hunting rifle—using his hunting rifle might wind up in the papers too, you see. But when she got to John's that Saturday morning she didn't wait for him to let her into the house. She didn't wait to hear him speak a single word. It isn't that they had an argument and it escalated and she shot him. Seeing his face was all it took—right there in the front doorway, she pulled the trigger twice and he was dead. She told me, 'He wanted mayhem, so I gave him mayhem.'"

"Does the little girl know anything?"

"She hasn't been told yet. That's not going to be easy. Nothing about this is going to be easy. The late Dr. Van Buren made sure of that. The suffering that's going to be Alison's is unimaginable to me."

Axler repeated to himself for days afterward, *The*

suffering that's going to be Alison's. It was probably the very thought that had driven Sybil to murder her husband—thereby enlarging Alison's suffering forever.

ONE NIGHT IN BED Pegeen said to him, "I've found a girl for you. She's on the Prescott swim team. I swim with her in the afternoon. Lara. How would you like me to bring you Lara?"

She was slowly rising and falling above him and all the lights were out, though the room was dimly lit by the full moon shining through the branches of the tall trees out back of the house.

"Tell me about Lara," he said.

"Oh, you'd like her all right."

"Obviously you do already."

"I watch her in the pool. I watch her in the locker room. A rich kid. A privileged kid. She's never known a minute's hardship. She's perfect. Blond. Crystal blue eyes. Long legs. Strong legs. Perfect breasts."

"How perfect?"

"It makes you awfully hard to hear about Lara," she said.

"The breasts," he said.

"She's nineteen. They're solid and they're just up there. Her cunt is shaved and there's just a fringe of blond hair to either side."

"Who's fucking her? The boys or the girls?"

"I don't know yet. But somebody's been having some fun down there."

From then on Lara was with them whenever they wanted her.

"You're fucking her," Pegeen would say. "That's Lara's perfect little pussy."

"You fucking her too?"

"No. Just you. Close your eyes. You want her to make you come? You want Lara to make you come? All right, you blond little bitch—make him come!" Pegeen cried, and no longer did he have to tell her how to ride the horse. "Squirt it all over her. Now! Now! Yes, that's it—squirt in her face!"

They went to a local inn one night for dinner. From the rustic dining room you could see out over the road to a big lake emblazoned by the sunset. She wore her newest clothes; they'd gone shopping for them on an impulsive visit to New York the week before: a little clinging black jersey skirt, a red cashmere sleeveless shell with a red cashmere cardigan knotted over her shoulders, sheer black stockings, a soft leather shoulder bag trimmed with small leather streamers, and on her feet a pair of pointy black slingbacks cut to show the cleavage of the foot. She looked soft and curvaceous and enticing, red above and everything black from the waist down, and she carried herself with such casual comfort that she might have been dressing like that all her life. She wore the shoulder bag, as the saleswoman had suggested, with the strap slung across her body like a bandolier and the bag riding her hip.

To try to prevent his back from locking and his leg from going dead, it was his habit to get up and walk around two or three times during a meal, and so after the main course and before dessert Axler stood and for the second time strolled through the restaurant and across the inn's public sitting room and into the bar. There he saw an attractive young woman drinking by herself. She must have been in her twenties, and from the way she was talking to the bartender he could tell she was a little drunk. He smiled when she looked his way and, so as to prolong his stay, he asked the bartender if he knew the ball score. Then he asked her if she was local or staying at the inn. She said she had just taken a job at the antique shop down the road and had stopped in after work for a drink. He asked if she knew anything about antiques, and she said her parents owned an antique shop farther upstate. She had been working at a shop in Greenwich Village for three years and had decided to get away from the city and try her luck in Washington County. He asked how long she'd been out here, and she said she'd arrived only the month before. He asked what she was drinking, and when she told him he said, "Next one's on me," and indicated to the bartender that he should put the drink on his tab.

When dessert arrived he said to Pegeen, "There's a girl at the bar getting drunk."

"What does she look like?"

"Like she can take care of herself."

"You want to?"

"If you do," he said.

"How old is she?" she said.

"I'd say twenty-eight. You'd be in charge. You and the green cock."

"You'd be in charge," she said to him. "You and the real cock."

"We'd be in charge together," he said.

"I want to see her," she said.

He paid the bill and they left the restaurant and went to stand in the doorway of the bar. He stood behind Pegeen with his arms encircling her. He could feel her trembling with excitement as she watched the girl drinking at the bar. Her trembling thrilled him. It was as though they had merged into one maniacally tempted being.

"You like her?" he whispered.

"She looks as if she could be quite indecent, given half a chance. She looks like she's ready for a life of crime."

"You want to take her home."

"She's not Lara but she'd do."

"What if she vomits in the car?"

"You think she's about to?"

"She's been at it a long time. When she passes out at the house, how do we get rid of her?"

"Murder her," Pegeen said.

While still closely holding Pegeen in front of him, he called across the bar, "Do you need a ride, young lady?"

"Tracy."

"Do you need a ride, Tracy?"

"I've got my car," Tracy replied.

"Are you in any shape to drive it? I can drop

you off at home." Pegeen was still quivering in his arms. She's a cat, he thought, before the cat pounces, the falcon before it soars from the falconer's wrist. The animal you can control—until you let it loose. He thought, I am providing her Tracy the way I give her the clothes. Everyone felt emboldened with Lara because there was no Lara there and so no consequences. This he knew to be different. It dawned on him that he was ceding all the power to Pegeen.

"I can get my husband to pick me up," Tracy said.

He'd noticed earlier that she wore no wedding ring. "No, let us drive you. Where do you want to go?"

Tracy mentioned a town twelve miles to the west.

The bartender, who knew Axler lived in the opposite direction, went about his job as if he were a deaf-mute. Because of Axler's movies, practically everyone in the rural town of nine hundred knew who he was, though few had any idea that his reputation rested on his lifetime's achievement on the stage. The drunken young woman paid her bill and climbed off the stool and grabbed her jacket to leave. She was taller than he'd imagined and larger, too—a stray perhaps, but no waif—a buxom blond with an extensive body and a kind of ready-made Nordic prettiness. In all, a coarser, commonplace version of stately Louise.

He put Tracy in the back seat with Pegeen and drove them along the dark country roads, empty of traffic, to his house. It was as though they were abducting her. The swiftness with which Pegeen moved did not take him by surprise. She was not constrained by inhibition or fear as she had been when she'd gotten her haircut, and he was already enthralled merely by what he could hear from the back of the car. In the bedroom at home Pegeen emptied onto the bed her plastic bag of implements, among them the toy-like cat-o'-nine-tails with its very soft, thin wisps of black unknotted leather.

AXLER WONDERED what was going on in Tracy's mind. She gets into a car with two people she's never seen before, they drive her to a house on a dirt road deep in the country, and then she steps out of the car into a three-ring circus. She may be drunk but she's also young. How oblivious to risk can she be? Or do Pegeen and I inspire trust? Or is risk what Tracy's looking for? Or is she too drunk to care? He wondered if she had ever done anything like this before. He wondered again why she was doing it now. It didn't make sense that this Tracy should fall into their laps to do all of the Lara-like stuff they'd been dreaming excitedly about in bed. Though what did make sense? His being unable to go out and act on a stage? His having been a psychiatric inpatient? His conducting a love affair with a lesbian whom he'd first seen nursing at her mother's breast?

When a man gets two women together, it is not unusual for one of the women, rightly or wrongly feeling neglected, to wind up crying in a corner of the room. From how this was going so far, it looked as though the one who'd wind up crying in the corner would be him. Yet as he watched from the far side of the bed, he did not feel painfully overlooked. He had let Pegeen appoint herself ringmaster and would not participate until summoned. He would watch without interfering. First Pegeen stepped into the contraption, adjusted and secured the leather straps, and affixed the dildo so that it jutted straight out. Then she crouched above Tracy, brushing Tracy's lips and nipples with her mouth and fondling her breasts, and then she slid down a ways and gently penetrated Tracy with the dildo. Pegeen did not have to force her open. She did not have to say a word—he imagined that if either one of them did begin to speak, it would be in a language unrecognizable to him. The green cock plunged in and out of the abundant naked body sprawled beneath it, slow at first, then faster and harder, then harder still, and all of Tracy's curves and hollows moved in unison with it. This was not soft porn. This was no longer two unclothed women caressing and kissing on a bed. There was something primitive about it now, this woman-on-woman violence, as though, in the room filled with shadows, Pegeen were a magical composite of shaman, acrobat, and animal. It was as if she were wearing a mask on her genitals, a weird totem mask, that made her into what she was not and was not supposed to be. She could as well have been a crow or a coyote, while simultaneously Pegeen Mike. There was something dangerous about it. His heart thumped with excitement—the god Pan looking on from a distance with his spying, lascivi-ous gaze.

It was English that Pegeen spoke when she looked over from where she was, now resting on her back beside Tracy, combing the little black cat-o'-nine-tails through Tracy's long hair, and, with that kid-like smile that showed her two front teeth, said to him softly, "Your turn. Defile her." She took Tracy by one shoulder, whispered "Time to change masters," and gently rolled the stranger's large, warm body toward his. "Three children got together," he said, "and decided to put on a play," whereupon his performance began.

AROUND MIDNIGHT they drove Tracy back to the lot beside the inn where she'd left her car.

"You two do this often?" Tracy asked from the back seat, where she lay encircled by Pegeen's arms.

"No," Pegeen said. "Do you?"

"Never in my life."

"So what do you think?" asked Pegeen.

"I can't think. My head's too crammed with everything to think. I feel tripped out. I feel like I've taken drugs."

"Where did you get the bravado for this?" Pegeen asked her. "The booze?"

"Your clothes. The way you looked. I thought, I

have nothing to fear. Tell me, is he that actor?" Tracy asked Pegeen, as though he weren't in the car.

"He is," Pegeen said.

"That's what the bartender said. Are you an actress?" she asked Pegeen.

"Off and on," Pegeen said.

"It was crazy," Tracy said.

"It was," Pegeen replied, the wielder of the cat-o'-nine-tails and connoisseur of the dildo, who was herself no dabbler, who had indeed carried things to the limit.

Tracy kissed Pegeen passionately when they said goodnight. Passionately Pegeen returned the kiss and stroked her hair and clutched her breasts, and in the parking lot beside the inn where they'd all met, the two momentarily clung together. Then Tracy got into her car, and before she drove off, he heard Pegeen tell her, "See you soon."

They drove home with Pegeen's hand down in his pants. "The smell," she said, "it's on us," while Axler thought, I miscalculated—I didn't think it through. He was the god Pan no longer. Far from it.

WHILE PEGEEN SHOWERED, he sat downstairs in the kitchen and had a cup of tea as if nothing had happened, as if another ordinary night had been passed at home. The tea, the cup, the saucer, the sugar, the cream—all answered a need for the matter-of-fact.

"I want to have a child." He imagined Pegeen speaking those words. He imagined her telling him when she came into the kitchen after the shower, "I want to have a child." He was imagining the least likely thing that might happen, which was why he was imagining it; he was out to force his foolhardiness back into a domestic container.

"With whom?" he imagined himself asking her.

"With you. You are the choice of my life."

"As your family has duly warned you, I'm closing in on seventy. When the child is ten I'll be seventy-five, seventy-six. By then I may not be your choice. I'll be in a wheelchair with this spine of mine, if not already dead."

"Forget about my family," he imagined her saying. "I want you to be the father of my child."

"Are you going to keep this a secret from Asa and Carol?"

"No. All that's over. You were right. Louise did me a favor with that phone call. No more secrecy. They'll have to live with things as they are."

"And where did this desire come from to mother a child?"

"From becoming what I've become for you."

He imagined himself saying, "Who could have foreseen this evening taking this turn?"

"Not at all," he imagined Pegeen replying. "It's the next step. If we're to continue, I want three things. I want you to have back surgery. I want you to resume your career. I want you to impregnate me."

"You want a lot."

"Who taught me to want a lot?" he imagined her saying. "That's my proposal for a real life. What more can I offer?"

"Back surgery is very tricky. The doctors I've seen say it would do no good in my case."

"You can't go on locked up with that pain. You can't go on hobbling around forever."

"And my career is trickier still."

"No," he imagined her saying, "it's a matter of adopting a plan to end the uncertainty. A bold long-term plan."

"That's all that's required," he imagined himself answering.

"Yes. It's time to be bold with yourself."

"If anything, it sounds like it's time to be cautious."

But because in her company he had begun to be rejuvenated, because he had done everything in his power to get himself to believe that she who'd begun by offering him a glass of water—only to go from there to pulling off the feat of feats, the sex-change act—could indeed make contentment real with him, he thought the most hopeful thoughts he could. In this kitchen reverie of the rectified life he imagined himself seeing an orthopedist who sent him for an MRI and after that for a presurgical myelogram and after that for surgery. Meanwhile he would have contacted Jerry Oppenheim and told him that if anyone wanted to offer him a role, he was available to work again. Then, still at the kitchen table exciting himself by elaborating these thoughts while Pegeen finished showering upstairs, he imagined Pegeen having a healthy baby the very month that he opened at the Guthrie Theater in the role of James Tyrone. He would have found Vincent Daniels's card where he had left it as a bookmark in the copy of *Long Day's Journey*. He would have gone to see Vincent Daniels with the script and they would have worked together every

day until they found the way to get him to stop dis-
trusting himself, so that when he went onstage at
the Guthrie on opening night, the lost magic returned, and he knew while the words were flying so
naturally, so effortlessly out of his mouth that he
was in the midst of a performance as good as any he
had ever given and that maybe being incapacitated
for so long, however painful, hadn't been the worst
thing that could have happened. Now the audience
believed him anew in every moment. Where, previ-
ously, confronting the scariest part of acting—the
line, saying something, saying something sponta-
neously with freedom and ease—he had felt himself
naked, without the protection of any approach,
now everything was once again emanating from instinct and he needed no other means of approach.
The stretch of bad luck was over. The self-inflicted
torment was over. He had recovered his confidence, the grief was displaced, the abominable fear
was dispelled, and everything that had fled him was
back where it belonged. The reconstruction of a
life had to begin somewhere, and for him it had
started with falling for Pegeen Stapleford, amaz-
ingly just the woman to have recruited for the job.

It seemed to him now that the kitchen scenario

was no longer the aery tale with which he'd begun but that he was imagining a new possibility, a reclamation of exuberance that it was his intention to fight for and to implement and to enjoy. Axler felt the determination that was originally his when he came to New York to audition at the age of twenty-two.

THE NEXT MORNING, as soon as Pegeen had left to drive back to Vermont, he called a hospital in New York and asked for a doctor with whom he could consult about the genetic hazards of fathering a child at sixty-five. He was referred to the office of a specialist and given an appointment for the following week. He said nothing about any of this to Pegeen.

The hospital was far uptown, and after parking the car in a garage, he made his way with mounting excitement to the doctor's office. He was given the usual medical forms to fill out and then greeted by a Filipino man of about thirty-five who said he was Dr. Wan's assistant. There was a windowed room off the waiting area, and the assistant led him there so that they could be alone. It seemed a room designed to be used by children, with low tables and small chairs scattered about and children's drawings pinned to one wall. The two of them sat at one of the tables and the assistant began to ask him about himself and his family and the diseases they had suffered from and the diseases they had died of. The doctor's assistant recorded the answers on a sheet of paper printed with the skeleton of a family tree. Axler told him as much as he knew from as far back as his knowledge of the family extended. Then the assistant took a second sheet and asked about the family of the prospective mother. Axler could tell him only that Pegeen's parents were both living; he knew nothing about their medical histories or those of Pegeen's aunts, uncles, grandparents, and great-grandparents. The assistant asked for her family's country of origin, as he had asked for Axler's, and, having recorded the information, told Axler that he would give all the data to Dr. Wan and that after he and the doctor had conferred, she would come out to talk to Axler.

Alone in the room, Axler felt ecstatic with the return of his force and his naturalness and the abandonment of his humiliation and the end of his disappearance from the world. This wasn't reverie any longer; the revitalization of Simon Axler was truly under way. And under way in this room full of children's furniture, of all places. The scale of the furniture reminded him of the art therapy session at Hammerton, when he and Sybil Van Buren had been given crayons and paper in order to draw pictures for their therapist. He remembered how he had obediently set to coloring with the crayons like the child he'd once been in kindergarten class. He remembered the mortifying consequences of having ended up in Hammerton, how every trace of assuredness had vanished; he remembered how all he found to deliver him from a pervasive sense of defeat and dread was the conversation that he listened to in the rec room after dinner, the stories of those among the hospitalized infatuated still with how they had tried to kill themselves. Now, however, a huge man sitting awkwardly amid these little tables and chairs, he was at one with the actor, conscious of the achievement behind him and convinced that life could begin again.

DR. WAN was a small, slender young woman who said that she would, of course, need Pegeen's history too, but that she could begin at least to address his fears about birth defects in the offspring of aging fathers. She told him that although the ideal age for men to father children is their twenties, and although the risk of passing on genetic vulnerability or developmental disorders like autism is significantly increased after forty, and although older men had more sperm with damaged DNA than younger men, the odds of fathering normal offspring without birth defects were not necessarily dire for a man of his age and health, especially as some, though not all, birth defects could be detected during pregnancy. "The testicular cells that give rise to sperm divide every sixteen days," Dr. Wan explained to him while they sat across from each other at the little table. "This means that the cells have split about eight hundred times by age fifty. And with each cell division, the chance increases for errors in the sperm's DNA." Once Pegeen had provided her with the other half of the story, she could more fully evaluate their situation and work with them together should they wish to proceed further. She gave him her card along with a pamphlet that spelled out in detail the nature and risk of birth defects. She also explained that there might be decreased fertility at his age, and so, at his request, she provided him with a referral to a laboratory to have a sperm analysis. That way they could determine if there was likely to be any difficulty with conception. "There can be a problem," she told him, "of sperm count, of motility, or morphology." "I understand," he said and, to express an uncontrollable sense of gratitude, reached out to clutch her hand. The doctor smiled at him as if she were the older of the two and said, "Call me if you have questions."

Back at home, he had an enormous urge to phone Pegeen and tell her of the great idea that had taken hold of him and what he had done about it. But that conversation would have to wait until they were together the following weekend and had hours and hours to talk. Alone in bed that night, he read the pamphlet Dr. Wan had given him. "It takes healthy sperm to make a healthy baby . . . About 2 to 3 percent of all babies are born with a major birth defect . . . More than 20 rare but devastating genetic disorders have been linked to aging fathers . . . The older a man is when he conceives a child, the more likely his partner is to miscarry . . . Older fathers are more likely to have children with autism, schizophrenia, and Down syndrome . . ." He went through the pamphlet once and then again, and sobering as he found the information, mindful as he now was of the risks, he would not be dissuaded from his plans by what he read. Instead, too excited to sleep, thinking something wonderful was happening, he found himself down in the living room, further enlivened by listening to music, and, along with feelings of fearlessness such as he had not known for years, experiencing the deep biological longing for a child that is more commonly associated with a woman than with a man. Nothing about their being together seemed improbable any longer. She had to go with him to see Dr. Wan. Once everyone had the whole story, the two of them would soberly assess what should come next.

He had planned to begin the conversation after dinner on Friday evening. But when Pegeen arrived for the weekend late Friday afternoon, she went off to her study with a slew of student exams to mark and left it to him to make dinner. And after dinner she withdrew again to the study to grade more exams. He thought, Let her get everything done now. Then we'll have the weekend to talk.

In bed in the dark—two weeks to the day after the tryst with Tracy—when he began to kiss and to fondle Pegeen, she pulled away and said, "My heart's not in it tonight." "All right," he said and, unable to arouse her, rolled over to his side but without relinquishing her hand, which he held on to with his own hand—the hand that still wanted to touch everything—until she'd fallen asleep. When he awakened in the middle of the night, he wondered, What did it mean that her heart wasn't in it, why had she been so unwilling to be near him from the moment she'd arrived?

He found out first thing the next morning, before he even had a chance to begin to tell her about his meeting with Dr. Wan and all that lay behind that meeting and all that potentially lay ahead of them; he found out that in going to see Dr. Wan he hadn't so much educated himself in order to avoid doing something rash as to dig himself deeper into an unreal world.

"This is the end," she said to Axler at the breakfast table. Each was seated across from the other in the very chairs as when she had told him in months gone by that they had already taken the risk.

"End of what?" he asked.

"Of this."

"But *why?*"

"It's not what I want. I made a mistake."

So began the end, as abruptly as that, and it concluded some thirty minutes later with Pegeen at the front door clutching her full duffle bag and Axler in tears. This was the very antithesis of his expectations that night in the kitchen two weeks back. The very antithesis of his expectations when he'd gone to see Dr. Wan. Everything he wanted, she was preventing him from having!

And she was crying now as well; it was not as easy to pull off as it had seemed in the first moment at the kitchen table. But still she would not be budged, and however much he wept, she remained silent. The picture she made at the front door, back in her boy's zippered red jacket and holding her duffle bag, expressed it all: this form of hardship she could endure. She was not about to sit down over a cup of coffee and have a heart-to-heart talk that would lead to a rapprochement. She wanted only to be free of him and to satisfy the common enough human wish to move on and try something else.

"You cannot nullify everything!" he shouted angrily, and with that Pegeen, the mightier of the two, opened the door.

At last she spoke, sobbing. "I tried to be perfect for you."

"What the hell does that mean? Was it ever a matter of being perfect? 'Don't pull away from me. I love this, and I don't want it to stop.' I was idiot enough to believe what you said. I was idiot enough to think you were doing what you wanted to do."

"It was what I wanted to do. I wanted so much to see if I could do it."

"So it was an experiment, right down to the end. Another adventure for Pegeen Mike—like picking up a pitcher on a softball team."

"I can't be a substitute for your acting anymore."

"Oh, don't pull that! That's disgusting!"

"But it's true! I'm what you have instead of that! I'm supposed to make up for that!"

"That's the most ludicrous bullshit I've ever heard. And you know it. Go, Pegeen! If that's your vindication, go! 'We took the risk.' *I* took the risk! You just said whatever you thought I wanted to hear so that you could get what you wanted as long as you wanted it."

"I did no such thing!" she cried.

"It's Tracy, isn't it?"

"What is?"

"You're dumping me for Tracy!"

"I'm not, Simon! No!"

"You're not leaving me because I don't have a job! You're leaving me for that girl! You're going to that girl!"

"Where I go is my business. Oh, just *let* me go!"

"Who's holding you back? Not me! Never!" He pointed at the duffle bag into which she had crammed all the new clothes of hers that had been hanging in his closets and folded in his bureau drawers. "Pack your sex toys?" he asked. "Remember your harness?"

She did not answer, but the emotion flashing through her was hatred, or so he understood the look in her eyes.

"Yes," he said, "take the tools of your trade and go. Now your parents can sleep at night—you're no longer with an old man. Now there's no interloper between you and your father. You're unburdened of your impediment. No more admonitions from home. Safely returned to your original position. Good. Go on to the next one. I never had the strength for you anyway."

A man's way is laid with a multitude of traps, and Pegeen had been the last. He'd stepped hungrily into it and taken the bait like the most craven captive on earth. There was no other way for it to wind up, and yet he was the last to find out. Improbable? No, predictable. Abandoned after so long? Clearly not so long for her as for him. Everything enchanting about her was gone, and in the time it had taken her to say "This is the end," he was condemned to his hole with the six sticks, alone and emptied of the desire to live.

She left in her car, and the process of collapse took less than five minutes, a collapse from a fall brought on himself and from which there was now no recovery.

HE WENT UP to the attic and sat there for a whole day and well into the night, preparing to pull the trigger of his shotgun and intermittently ready to rush down the stairs and wake Jerry Oppenheim at home, ready to call Hammerton and speak to his doctor, ready to dial 911.

And at a dozen different moments throughout the day, ready to call Lansing and tell Asa what a treacherous son of a bitch he was to have turned Pegeen against him. That was how it had happened, he was sure. Pegeen had been right all along to want to keep the news of their affair from her family. "Because they've known you so long," she'd explained to him when he'd asked why she preferred to keep him a secret. "Because you're all the same age." Had he made the trip to Michigan when he first suggested to Pegeen his going out there to talk to Asa, he might perhaps have had a chance to win. But to phone Asa now would accomplish nothing. Pegeen was gone. Gone to Tracy. Gone to Lara. Gone to the pitcher with the ponytail. Wherever she was, he no longer had to worry about the genetic hazards of being an aging father with testicular cells that had already divided well over eight hundred times.

By dinnertime he could restrain himself no longer and, carrying the gun with him, he came down from the attic to the phone.

Carol answered.

"It's Simon Axler."

"Why, yes. Hello, Simon."

"Let me speak to Asa." His voice was trembling and his heartbeat had quickened. He had to sit in a kitchen chair to continue. It was very like the way he'd felt in Washington the last time he had tried to go out on a stage to perform. And yet none of this might be happening if only Louise Renner hadn't made that vengeful midnight phone call telling the Staplefords about their daughter and him.

"Are you all right?" Carol asked.

"Not really. Pegeen has walked out on me. Let me speak to Asa."

"Asa is still at the theater. You could try his office there."

"Put him on, Carol!"

"I just told you, he's not home yet."

"Isn't it wonderful news? Isn't it a great relief? You no longer have to worry about your daughter tending to the needs of a feeble old man. You no longer have to worry that she'll have to be keeper to a madman and nursemaid to an invalid. But then I'm not telling you anything you don't know—I'm not telling you anything you didn't help to cook up."

"You're telling me that Pegeen has left you?"

"Let me speak to Asa."

There was a pause, and then, unlike him, with perfect composure, she said, "You can try to reach Asa at his office. I'll give you the number and you can call him there."

He did not know now, any more than when he decided to call, whether he was doing the right thing, the wrong thing, the weak thing, or the strong thing. He set the gun on the kitchen table and took down the number Carol gave him and hung up without saying anything further. If he were given this role to act in a play, how would he do it? How would he do the phone call? In a voice that was trembling or a voice that was firm? With wit or with savagery, renunciation or rage? He could no more figure out how to play the elderly lover abandoned by the mistress twenty-five years his junior than he'd been able to figure out how to play Macbeth. Shouldn't he just have blown his brains out while Carol was at the other end listening? Wouldn't *that* have been the best way to play it?

He could stop, of course. He could stop the madness right here. He wasn't going to win Pegeen back by going on to dial Asa's number, yet he dialed it. He wasn't trying to win her back. There was no winning her back. No, he simply would not be outmaneuvered and outwitted by a second-rate actor who held sway, with the second-rate actress who was his wife, over a regional theater in the middle of nowhere. The Staplefords couldn't make it on the stage in New York, they couldn't make it in film in California, so they're making great dramatic art, he thought, out beyond the corruptions of the commercial world. No, he would not be defeated by these two mediocrities. He would not be a boy overcome by her parents!

The phone rang only once before Asa answered and said hello.

"Just how did it benefit you," Axler began, seething, shouting resentfully, "to turn her against me? You couldn't stand that she was a lesbian in the first place. That's what she said—neither you nor Carol could bear it. You were appalled when she told you. Well, with me she had relinquished all that, with me she had opened herself to a new way of life— and was happy! You never saw the two of us together. Pegeen and I were *happy!* But instead of being grateful to me, you persuade her to pick up and leave! Even her going back to being a lesbian was preferable to her being with me! Why? Why? Explain this to me, please."

"First, Simon, you must calm down. I won't listen to a tirade."

"Do you have some special dislike of me dating back to the beginning? Is there envy here, Asa, or revenge perhaps, or jealousy? What harm have I done her? I'm sixty-six, I haven't been working, my spine's a problem—where is the horror in that? Where is the threat to your daughter in that? Did it prevent me from offering her anything she wanted? I gave Pegeen everything I possibly could! I tried to satisfy her in every conceivable way!"

"I'm sure you did. She said as much to Carol and me. No one could fault you for your generosity and no one has."

"You know she's left me."

"I do now."

"You didn't before?"

"No."

"I don't believe you, Asa."

"Pegeen does what she wants to do. She's done that all her life."

"Pegeen did what you wanted her to do!"

"I am well within my rights as a father to be concerned about a daughter and give counsel to her. I would be remiss if I didn't."

"But how could you 'give counsel' when you knew nothing about what was going on between us? All you had in your head was a vision of me, with all my renown, with all my success, stealing away what was rightfully yours! It wasn't fair, Asa, was it, that I should have Pegeen too!"

Shouldn't he have played that line for a laugh instead of delivering it in a fit of anger? Shouldn't he have been quietly sardonic, as though it were a deliberately needling overstatement rather than his sounding out of his mind? Oh, play it however you like, Axler told himself. Probably you're playing it for laughs anyway without your even knowing it.

He detested his tears but he was all at once crying again, crying from the shame and the loss and the rage all tangled together, and so he hung up on the call to Asa that he never should have made in the first place. Because it was he, finally, who was responsible for what had happened. Yes, he had tried to satisfy her in every imaginable way, and so, idiotically, he'd introduced Tracy into their life and undone everything. But then how could he have foreseen that? Tracy was party to a game, a beguiling sex game of the kind that any number of couples play for diversion and excitement. How could he foresee a pickup at the bar would end with his losing Pegeen for good? Would someone smarter have known better? Or was this a continuation of the turn his luck had taken playing Prospero and Macbeth? Was all of this owing to stupidity, or was it just his way of digging himself one layer deeper down into the final demise?

And who was this Tracy? The new salesgirl at a rural antique shop. A lonesome drunk at a country inn. Who was she compared with him? This was impossible! How could he be overthrown for Tracy? How could he be defeated by Asa? Was Pegeen leaving him for Tracy because subterraneanly it hurled his little girl back into Papa's arms? And suppose she wasn't leaving him for Tracy. Or leaving him because of her family's objections. Then what had made him repugnant to her? Why was he suddenly taboo?

He carried the gun into Pegeen's study and stood there looking at the room that she had stripped of Victoria's wallpaper and then painted a shade of peach, the room that she had made into hers just as he, holding nothing back, had invited her to make him into hers. He suppressed an urge to fire a shot into the back of her desk chair and sat in it instead. He saw for the first time that all the books she'd brought from home had been removed from the bookcase beside the desk. When did she empty those shelves? How far back did the decision to leave him go? Had it been there all along, even while she was stripping these walls?

Now he suppressed the urge to fire the gun into the bookcase. Instead he ran his hand over the empty shelves that had housed her books, and tried in vain to think of what he could have done differently over all these months that would have made her want to stay.

After what must have been at least an hour, he decided not to be found dead in Pegeen's room, in Pegeen's chair. The culprit wasn't Pegeen. The failures were his, as was the bewildering biography on which he was impaled.

WHEN, LONG AFTER calling Asa, sometime around midnight—having retreated back to the attic several hours before—he could not pull the trigger even after he had gone so far as to place the barrel of the gun inside his mouth, he challenged himself to remember tiny Sybil Van Buren, that conventional suburban housewife weighing less than a hundred pounds who finished what she set out to do, who took on the gruesome role of a murderer, and succeeded at it. Yes, he thought, if she could summon up the force to do something so terrible to the husband who was her demon, then I can at least do this to myself. He imagined the steeliness that went into her carrying her plan to the brutal end: the ruthless madness that she'd mobilized in leaving the two small children at home, her driving single-mindedly to the estranged husband's house, her mounting the stairs, ringing the bell, raising the rifle, and, when he opened the door, without hesitation her firing twice at point-blank range—if she could do that, I can do this!

Sybil Van Buren became the benchmark of courage. He repeated to himself the inspiring formula to action, as though a simple word or two could get him to accomplish the most unreal of all things: *if she could do that, I can do this, if she could do that* . . . until finally it occurred to him to pretend that he was committing suicide in a play. In a play by Chekhov. What could be more fitting? It would constitute his return to acting, and, preposterous, disgraced, feeble little being that he was, a lesbian's thirteen-month mistake, it would take everything in him to get the job done. To succeed one last time to make the imagined real he would have to pretend that the attic was a theater and that he was Konstantin Gavrilovich Treplev in the concluding scene of *The Seagull.* In his mid-twenties, when, as a theatrical prodigy, he accomplished everything he tried and achieved everything he wanted, he had played the part of Chekhov's aspiring young writer who feels a failure at everything, desperate with defeat at work and love. It was in an Actors Studio Broadway production of *The Seagull,* and it marked his first big New York success, making him the most promising young actor of the season, full of certainty and a sense of singularity, and leading to every unforeseeable contingency.

If she could do that, I can do this.

There was a note of eight words found alongside him when his body was discovered on the floor of the attic by the cleaning woman later that week. "The fact is, Konstantin Gavrilovich has shot himself." It was the final line spoken in *The Seagull.* He had brought it off, the well-established stage star, once so widely heralded for his force as an actor, whom in his heyday people would flock to the theater to see.